"Undress me, Felicity."

Steven held his arms wide in a gesture of invitation.

With trembling fingers, Felicity obeyed.

It was incomparably erotic, she found, helping this strong, virile man out of his clothes. As she bent her head to unbuckle his belt she felt the light touch of his injured fingers in her hair, as though he just couldn't resist this caress. When she looked up, he smiled, his amazing eyes catching glints of light from the fire.

She pulled his shirt out of the corduroy pants and slipped it down his shoulders and bare, muscular arms. When she lifted her eyes again she was mesmerized by the look on his face. Still, he didn't speak.

As if in a dream, she pulled his shirt off and dropped it to the floor. Then she turned to the zipper of his pants, sliding it down....

He laughed softly at the expression on her face. "Don't look so surprised," he said. "You should have known what you'd find...."

Maggie Davis has been a radio talk-show hostess, a copywriter for television and radio and a contributor to magazines such as *Cosmopolitan* and *Ladies Home Journal*. She has even taught writing courses at Yale University. Since 1963 she's penned a dozen general-list titles for a number of mainstream publishers. But Maggie really wanted to write short romantic comedies for Harlequin, too. So, with *Dreamboat*, she enters the romance genre for the first time. Temptation is proud to publish the delightful work of this prestigious and versatile author.

Dreamboat

MAGGIE DAVIS

Harlequin Books

TORONTO • NEW YORK • LONDON
AMSTERDAM • PARIS • SYDNEY • HAMBURG
STOCKHOLM • ATHENS • TOKYO • MILAN

For Linda Benson,
who made me write it

Published October 1989

ISBN 0-373-25372-9

1

HE WAS NOT ONLY a blind date, Felicity saw to her dismay, he was a blind date with a *Ferrari*. The sleek, red car was drawn up in the driveway beside her own scruffy 1975 Dodge station wagon, which still held, unfortunately, the larger-than-life-sized papier-mâché Cookie Monster from the nursery school's Thanksgiving play.

He was also, Felicity observed as she rubbed a clear place on the steamy window glass to see him, too gorgeous to be believed. So all the rumors were true! As he exited from the low-slung Ferrari he carefully snapped open a large black umbrella to protect his beautiful tuxedo from the downpour.

Felicity saw Dr. Steven Cambridge hesitate, scowling, as he surveyed the driveway's deep puddles and little Bobby Kendrick's overturned tricycle. From the expression on his face she couldn't help wondering how it dared rain when he obviously didn't want it to.

But he certainly was a "dreamboat," she admitted, impressed. This was her first sight of the prestigious new head of Griffin Memorial's neurological center. She felt her throat muscles tighten.

Drat this whole ridiculous thing! She was nervous, and who wouldn't be? At twenty-eight years of age she was too busy, too committed, she told herself, too *fulfilled* for the hassle of blind dates.

Besides, she didn't *want* to go to Griffin Hospital Board's annual dinner dance at the country club with Dr. Steven Gorgeous; that had been someone else's idea. She was hardly, Felicity told herself crossly, "dreamboat" date material, and certainly no Miss Griffin County beauty contest winner, even quite attractively dressed in her one and only formal gown, a green satin crepe that had once belonged to her younger, more socially active sister.

In the rain-darkened window glass Felicity could see her reflection and knew the wet weather was making her red hair knot up into frizzy curls. The color of her hair was plain red—not chestnut, Titian, mahogany, or strawberry blond. No one called her "Red" anymore, not since grammar school, but at five foot ten and with a healthy number of freckles like paint flecks over the bridge of a very ordinary-looking nose, she certainly didn't add up to anything exquisitely beautiful, either.

Dr. Cambridge, Felicity saw as he bent to drag Bobby Kendrick's tricycle out of his way, was tall, at least several inches over six feet. His rain-sprinkled hair was light brown, liberally sunstreaked with strands of pale burnished gold, and his face was square-jawed, with a rather long, patrician nose. Actually he was a sort of riveting mix of a young Robert Redford with a slight touch, now, of a grimly dutiful Michael Douglas.

Why me? Felicity couldn't help thinking.

She saw him give a passing, disapproving glance at the back of her station wagon and its rear window sign, Felicity's Gingerbread House Child-care Center, which hung over the heads of Big Bird and the Cookie Monster. *Or for that matter,* she thought, sighing, *why Dr. Steven Cambridge?* Who, from the look of him, didn't want to be here any more than she did.

The answer, of course, was that they'd both been forced into this blind date in a nice way, by well-meaning people, because the First Griffin Bank and Trust Company held the mortgage on owner-operated Felicity's Gingerbread House Child-care Center. And Harry Tate Calloway, Sr., the bank's chairman of the board, was an ardent financial supporter of Griffin Memorial Hospital and most particularly his own pet project, the Harry Tate Calloway Neurological Clinic and Teaching Center—to which Dr. Steven Cambridge currently owed his recent appointment, his glorious future and last but not least, his very generous salary.

From the kitchen window she saw Dr. Cambridge hesitate between the path to the front door and the well-traveled rear door just off the driveway. From his expression Dr. Cambridge clearly didn't like elderly, somewhat rundown Georgia houses where one entered from the friendly, more accessible rear.

Wait until he gets a look at me, Felicity thought. She didn't remotely resemble the Atlanta television news anchorwomen, professional models and post-debutantes that local gossip said Dr. Cambridge had been dating. Unfortunately, Martha Calloway had her own theories about the women to whom their brilliant young neurosurgeon should be attracted.

"Do they still call them 'dreamboats'?" the banker's wife had wanted to know. "I mean, really good-looking men like Stevie Cambridge?"

"Well, 'hunks,' I guess, is more up-to-date," Felicity had answered uneasily.

At lunch in Atlanta's Capital City Club the look on Martha Calloway's face was all too familiar: the same avidly helpful expression Felicity was used to seeing on the faces of her sisters and friends since the disaster of her broken engagement with Michael Hanks some two years ago.

"A *what*?" Martha Calloway wanted to know.

Felicity spelled it out. But she dreaded what was coming. "H-u-n-k. As in 'magnificent hunk of man,' 'that's a beautiful hunk,' or even 'what a hunk.'"

When she'd accepted Martha Calloway's invitation to lunch she hadn't known the conversation was going to revolve around Martha Calloway's latest project, finding a "nice girl" for the brilliant young Dr. Steven Cambridge. Who, goodness only knows, looked as though he could take care of himself.

"Hunk? Oh, honey, I like that!" The other woman's bright gray eyes had twinkled enthusiastically. "That boy's picked all the wrong women to get engaged to, that's all."

"Women?" Felicity had said, alarmed. "You mean women, *plural*?"

"Only four, dear," Martha soothed her. "And they came and went just like that!" She snapped her fingers to illustrate. "That's not many in this day and age, now is it?"

Four was certainly too many as far as Felicity was concerned. She was still trying to recover from her one and only engagement a few years ago that had set some sort of record for middle Georgia's most bizarre and publicly humiliating betrothal, before it was called off. *Engagement* was a dirty word now, after Michael Hanks; Felicity had to admit she was definitely traumatized.

Even so, she could see how the wind was blowing. Martha Calloway was not only wife of one of the southeast's foremost multimillionaire philanthropists, she was a friend of Felicity's aunt—they'd gone to Randolph-Macon College together—and a pillar of middle Georgia Old Guard society. Martha Calloway's hobby, true to her background, was romance, if one could use such a comparatively frivolous term. Mrs. Harry Tate Calloway, senior, was an ironclad, stompdown, old-fashioned matchmaker. In her area of expertise the banker's wife could put computerized dating services out of business.

"Practically all of them," Martha Calloway continued, "were those little blond glamorous things without much personality. The last one was dumb as a bunny rabbit. Of course, with a brilliant young man like Steven Cambridge and a busy doctor, too, you just *know* he was bored stupid after the gloss wore off! I think what he needs," she said meaningfully, "is some intelligent, outgoing girl who's lots of fun." She deliberately did not look at Felicity. "One with some good old-fashioned *sense!*"

Felicity winced. Put that way, it sounded horrible. From what Martha Calloway said, Dr. Steven Cambridge was into dates that probably looked as though they'd just jumped out of the centerfold of *Playboy*. She was sure he wasn't ready to go cold turkey with Griffin's tall, lanky day-care and nursery school lady.

Martha Calloway thought otherwise.

"I know he hasn't got a date for the hospital dinner dance," the banker's wife said enthusiastically. "Harry Tate says that boy hasn't been having much of social life lately, his schedule's too heavy. But frankly I think Stevie's been moping about all those broken romances. We'll just have to get him out and circulating again!"

"I've been busy, too." Felicity wanted to get out of what she knew was coming up. "Uh, the Thanksgiving play at the—"

Martha Calloway ignored her protests. "You *have* got a long evening dress, haven't you, Felicity dear? If you haven't, my daughter Tootsie has a—"

"No—no, I'll manage!" Felicity didn't date enough to own an evening gown, but the last thing she wanted was to appear at the country club in one of Tootsie Calloway's hand-me-downs that half the town of Griffin would recognize. Better her own sister's castoffs sent in care packages from Chicago.

Now here she was, Felicity was thinking as she watched the broad-shouldered figure in his impeccable tuxedo start for the back of her house and the kitchen door, stuck with Martha Calloway's latest matchmaking project. And as a reward for dragging her off to the hospital board's annual dinner-dance bash, Dr. Cambridge got one Felicity Boardman, owner/ manager of a child-care center on which the First Griffin Bank and Trust Company held several outstanding notes. And who looked pretty passable, Felicity supposed, glancing at herself in the kitchen window, with her long red hair arranged in a braided coronet from which wisps of straggly little curls kept escaping thanks to the wet weather, dressed in a sparkling emerald beaded evening gown that once belonged to her younger sister.

But Felicity couldn't help wishing she were somewhere else—say, Alaska or mainland China. A knock at the back door interrupted her wry thoughts. *Well, here goes nothing*, she thought, opening the kitchen door.

From the expression on Dr. Cambridge's handsome face under a large, dripping black umbrella, he was not an enthusiastic date, either. "Miss Boardman?" he asked in a hollow voice.

No, Frankenstein's wife, she wanted to answer. Who did he think would be opening the back door of 75 Alsace Drive on a rainy November evening, all dressed up in a long green formal gown, anyway?

"Call me Felicity," she murmured. Remembering pompous hospital protocol, she couldn't resist being devilish. "And I'll call you Doctor Cambridge."

He didn't smile. "Yes," he said, staring at her gloomily.

Felicity felt a definite riffle of resentment make its way up her spine. Okay—Dr. Cambridge was young, brilliant, he had the whole Georgia medical profession at his feet with his outstanding brain research, and she wouldn't deny he was certainly a hunk if you liked them tall, sulky and dazzlingly handsome. She supposed she could even dredge up some sympathy for him under the circumstances: Dr. Cambridge looked to be the type of male who would fiercely resist having someone pick his dates for him, sight unseen.

Too darned bad, Felicity told herself as she picked up her raincoat from the kitchen chair. Her evening was pretty well shot, too. She'd planned to stay home herself and watch the old Gene Kelly movie, *Singing in the Rain*, on cable TV.

Felicity saw Dr. Cambridge's handsome face change from a look of reluctance to one of distaste as he eyed her old London Fog raincoat. "It's raining," she explained, unnecessarily.

He made a movement to help her. Then dropped his hands as he saw she'd managed to struggle into the coat by herself. "Yes, it's raining," he said. "And we're late."

"You got tied up," Felicity suggested. Actually she'd been standing by the kitchen window watching the driveway for more than forty-five minutes.

Dr. Cambridge drew his beautiful fine dark brows together in a slight scowl. "I'm always late," he muttered. "I got hung up in surgery."

Felicity stared at his unhappy chiseled features. She suddenly had a picture of Dr. Cambridge explaining to any one of his four former fiancées why he'd disappointed them by being late for a social engagement again because of some emergency at the hospital. It explained a lot.

She locked the back door as he held the umbrella over her, knowing it was going to be a long, dreary evening. But the Ferrari was as gorgeous as its owner, she noted as she slipped into the front seat. A definite change from the Porsches that usually filled the physicians' Reserved slots at the Griffin Hospital.

"Nice car," Felicity murmured as Steven Cambridge shoved the folded umbrella into the back seat and got in beside her.

"Umm," he responded, ungraciously.

We can scratch sports cars, Felicity thought, as a topic of conversation for the evening. Tennis anyone? It was either that or golf, she was sure. She never had time to play tennis anymore, and golf was an experience she'd carefully bypassed.

"So you run a nursery school," he said, making conversation, but not very interestedly. He started the Ferrari and turned to look out the rearview mirror.

Felicity had just opened her mouth, toying with the urge to reply that, no, actually she ran Griffin's first porno telephone service, but she never got to utter a word. As Dr. Cambridge backed the Ferrari slowly down the driveway there was a hideous squeal from somewhere under the car.

He flinched, visibly.

"Damn, what the hell was that?" he exclaimed as a dark, rain-bedraggled object shot out from under the Ferrari and streaked for the street. Dr. Cambridge spun the steering wheel just in time. The sports car mounted the grassy lawn to the left of Felicity's driveway. There was a distinct grating, grinding crunch under the rear axle, then it died away.

"That was my cat," Felicity said, letting go of the dashboard and taking a deep breath. "He likes to investigate strange cars, but I think you just gave him a nervous breakdown. And I think you just ran over little Bobby Kendrick's tricycle."

"The hell you say." He threw open the door on the driver's side and jumped out into the downpour. Felicity, grabbing the black umbrella from the floor of the back seat, was not far behind.

The only way anyone would know, Felicity thought as she stared through a curtain of heavy rain at the rear of the low-slung Ferrari, that a tricycle had just been mashed under the rear axle was that one small wheel— a warped oval shape—now protruded pathetically.

She glanced at the Kendricks' house next door. This was not a good time to mention that Walter Kendrick had a combative trigger temper, even when Bobby left his toys in the wrong driveway. Fortunately the Kendricks were not at home.

"Oh, damn, *damn*," he was saying. Heedless of his tuxedo and black evening oxfords, he splashed through the downpour, making a circuit of the Ferrari as he craned to get a look underneath. "Damn the goddamn thing!" Steven Cambridge was just as gorgeous when he was furious. "I don't dare try to move it, it will only damage my transmission!"

"That's ridiculous," Felicity said, calmly. "Transmissions are pretty indestruc—" She stopped short as Dr. Cambridge lifted his wet head and she met an enraged stare from cobalt-blue eyes.

"Ferrari transmissions are not indestructible," he said with stony fury. "They are *delicate*. That damned tricycle will tear up the housing if I move an inch and probably insert broken wheel spokes—" he looked anguished as he considered it "—handlebars, rubber—"

"Never mind," Felicity said quickly. Lord, the man was in love with his car! Chalk up *two* obsessions for the poor ex-fiancées—his demanding job and his expensive automobile! "Well, we could always, ah, call a cab."

She stopped. Getting one of Griffin's six taxicabs on a Saturday evening in a rainstorm was next to impossible. Even without a big dinner dance scheduled at the country club.

As she peered at him from under the shelter of his big black umbrella, Felicity could see Dr. Cambridge was not taking the evening's events very well. He was not only devastated by having a child's tricycle stuck under his car, he was also pretty well drenched—so carried away he didn't even notice he was standing, uncovered, in the pounding rainstorm. Felicity dreaded the moment when Dr. Gorgeous discovered he looked like a drowned rat. She vaguely remembered he was making a speech at the hospital-board dinner tonight.

He suddenly glanced at his expensive gold wristwatch. "Hell—we're late! I'm going to miss my speech!"

So it was true. Felicity sighed, inwardly. She had to think fast. "We could always take *my* car."

For a moment he visibly recoiled, then turned slowly to look at the 1975 Dodge station wagon. Over the sign, Felicity's Gingerbread House Child-care Center, the figures of Big Bird and the Cookie Monster gazed at them solemnly through the rain-wet rear window.

Felicity knew what was going through Dr. Cambridge's mind. Imagewise, driving up to the valet parking at the front door of the country club in her battered Dodge with larger-than-life papier-mâché animals in the back was not exactly the same as arriving elegantly in one's own $70,000 red Ferrari.

"Oh no, don't get Cookie Monster and Big Bird out of the back in this rain," Felicity cried quickly. "They'll melt!" She jogged anxiously after him as she made for the station wagon. "Don't do it," she begged. "Papier-mâché is so hard to work with, it took the nursery school weeks, we'll never duplic—"

"There isn't time, anyway," he growled. "I keep telling you, we're late." He held out his wet hand.

Felicity fished out the keys to the Dodge from her green satin evening purse. "Hadn't I better drive?" she said, giving them to him. "There's a little problem with the right front brake drum, it shakes when you—"

"Get in," he ordered as he slid rather squishily into the front seat, leaving Felicity and the umbrella in the driveway. "Dammit, how many times do I have to say we're late?"

Felicity made her way around to the passenger's side of the car and got in. The Dodge whined and coughed as he turned the key in the ignition, but the engine didn't catch.

"You have to pump the gas pedal," Felicity offered helpfully, "because—"

"All right, *all right*," he shouted over the sudden roar of the motor. "All I want to do is get there—do you *mind*?"

Felicity slumped in her seat and decided to say nothing for a while. The way things were going, she supposed there was a case for somebody as edgy and hard driving as Dr. Steven Cambridge to be just a little bit bad-tempered. Just as long as he didn't blame her!

They'd only gone a few blocks when he drew a deep breath, apparently deciding the worst was over, and reached up to run the fingers of one hand through his hair. He froze.

Felicity waited.

"Damn," she heard him say in tone of sheer incredulity, "I can't believe it! What the hell have we been doing?" He shook his hand, his fingertips spraying water. "I've got a speech to make! How did I get so abominably, soaking *wet*?"

2

EVERY SEAT at every pink-and-white decorated table in the country club ballroom was filled. A strolling accordionist played for cocktails, and by the time the guests took their seats, white-jacketed waiters were placing bottles of champagne on the tables next to the centerpieces of pink roses and white carnations.

The hospital fund's annual dinner dance was very festive, Felicity reflected; it was just too bad Dr. Steven Cambridge wasn't there to enjoy it. His empty seat beside her was as worrisome as a missing tooth. The guests were silently asking, as they looked up at the VIP table, what had become of their speaker for the evening? And who was this carrot-topped young woman in a green satin bugle-beaded evening dress sitting next to his empty chair? Some were looking at Felicity as though she might have done something sinister to the missing doctor.

Harry Tate Calloway noticed, too. The multimillionaire covered his mouth with his napkin as he rumbled, "Say, hon, do you suppose you ought to go and check on Stevie again? I'd go see how the boy's doing myself, but if I got down off this goldarned platform and took out of here people might think there was a fire or something, and start to leave."

A little far-fetched, but probably true, Felicity realized. Harry Tate Calloway was so powerful half the town would follow him anywhere, even out into a driving rainstorm. That was how many mortgages his bank controlled.

"I think he'll be along in a few minutes, Mr. Calloway." Felicity looked away from the accusing stare of a woman at a table just below. She was beginning to feel like an ax murderess.

Felicity knew very well what was keeping Dr. Steven Cambridge. He was sitting in his underwear, maybe still shivering, in the club manager's office.

Their arrival at the Griffin Golf and Country Club in Felicity's battered old Dodge station wagon had been about as bad as she had expected. The car-park attendant had done a comic double take at the life-sized replicas of Big Bird and the Cookie Monster in the back seat, his expression saying this wasn't exactly what one took to the country club for a gala formal event. Then when the attendant stepped on the gas the station wagon's engine died, blocking Cadillacs and Lincolns in front of the main entrance for several long minutes before he could get it cranked up again.

Dr. Cambridge, his teeth chattering with cold, looked, thanks to his soaking in Felicity's driveway, as though he'd fallen into a nearby lake. When the maître d'hotel saw him approaching the ballroom doors leaving a trail of wet footprints behind him, he'd promptly called the manager, who had tactfully steered him into the office to dry out.

When Felicity left them, Steven Cambridge's tuxedo jacket and pants were about to be rolled in dry towels by the service staff, then pressed with an iron. Since it was still pouring outside and the humidity remained high, there was little hope of getting him completely dry, but everyone from the club secretary to the Puerto Rican dishwasher, who was doing most of the ironing, were straining to ensure that the famous neurosurgeon was restored to something like his former heart-stopping perfection by the time the speech making began.

Felicity found her thoughts lingering over her last sight of Dr. Cambridge's long golden body folded in a chair in the manager's office. In spite of everything, he'd managed to look powerfully muscular and sexy in a pair of black stretch underwear briefs.

She jumped a little guiltily when Martha Calloway slid into the empty chair next to her.

"I hear your date had a bit of an accident." With sharp gray eyes the banker's wife's took in Felicity's coronet of red braids, dangling rhinestone earrings and the low-cut emerald satin gown. She nodded her approval. "Is everything going all right, dear?" She couldn't resist patting Felicity's hand. "Oh, girl—how lucky you are! He really *is* a dreamboat, isn't he?"

Felicity pulled her hand away. She wished Martha Calloway would stop acting as though she and Dr. Cambridge were already engaged.

"Well, uh," she stammered, "he did stand out in the rain too long."

That didn't sound right. But Felicity didn't want to launch into a long account of how Bobby Kendrick's tricycle managed to get stuck under Dr. Cambridge's Ferarri's rear axle. Not with half the hospital fund's patrons watching them from the tables below.

But Martha Calloway's matchmaking sixth sense had caught something. "There isn't anything wrong, is there? No, there couldn't be," she answered herself quickly, "he's such a nice young man, so brilliant and dedicated. High-strung men like that can be difficult to live with," Martha sighed. "Why, just look at my Harry!"

Felicity choked on a sip of water. Big, beefy, back-slapping Harry Tate Calloway, high-strung? At that moment they both saw Dr. Steven Cambridge making his way through the tables below. She braced herself. *Well*, was her first, rather panicky impression, *at least he's almost dry.*

That about took care of the positives. The negatives were there for all to see. The ironing-out in the club manager's office had left his tuxedo not so much badly wrinkled as spiritless, like a deflated party balloon. His bow tie had shrunk; it was now a knotted black string. He obviously hadn't gotten around to combing his hair, damp strands hung rakishly over his forehead. His chiseled features were pinched. He no longer looked as if he'd fallen into the nearest lake. Instead, in his ruined tuxedo he now had the disreputable air of a man returning from a three-day drunk.

Felicity squirmed. It would be a miracle if tense, irascible Dr. Steven Cambridge didn't somehow blame her for their disastrous evening. She braced herself for an arctic blast as soon as Dr. Cambridge sat down next to her.

Fortunately Harry Tate Calloway got to his feet almost immediately and launched into his introduction. The banker explained smoothly that Dr. Steven Cambridge had had car trouble on the way to the country club, and had gotten thoroughly soaked. With that point cleared up the audience managed to smile. The dinner guests sat back in their chairs and prepared themselves to be entertained by Dr. Cambridge.

As he moved to the podium Dr. Cambridge shot a ravenous glance at the desserts just being served. Felicity realized with a start that he'd obviously missed his dinner during his drying out in the club manager's office. Now that she considered it, he *did* look more hungry than nervous over any speech making.

From the moment Dr. Steven Cambridge began to speak it was obvious that if the fund raisers for Griffin Hospital had expected their star neurosurgeon to deliver a light, amusing talk full of little anecdotes about the funny things that happen in the operating room, they were going to be horrendously disappointed. The title of his talk, Dr. Steven Cambridge announced in his appealingly husky voice was, Multiple Manifestations of Brain Trauma in the Frontal Lobes.

Felicity sat entranced, only able to follow a few, nontechnical words. The rest of the guests only looked bemused. That is, at first.

On page two, he looked up from his prepared text long enough to give an impromptu description of the sound skull bones make when the surgeon bores into them, something he apparently found fascinating. Felicity saw guests push back their unfinished cherries jubilee. On the other side of Harry Tate Calloway the mayor's wife gave a little horror-struck gurgle.

Felicity propped one elbow on the table, chin in hand, as she regarded Dr. Steven Cambridge with new eyes. There was more to Griffin Hospital's new star than just a pretty face, she thought, admiringly. He had guts, she'd say that for him. Brain surgery for an after-dinner speech at the country club?

Maybe, she considered, he was so immersed in his work that he'd never stopped to consider a country club dinner-dance crowd's lack of appreciation for obscure cranial injury. But she had to admit that no matter what he was talking about, Dr. Cambridge was a treat to watch. Strands of damp golden hair fell over his forehead as his tall, broad-shouldered body leaned into his subject with all the concentration of a quarterback tensed for a power play.

The technical paper—it was hardly a speech, even Felicity realized that—was probably dazzling. It was also plain Dr. Cambridge had mentally faded out of the confines of the country-club ballroom into the world of his consuming passion.

Felicity dragged her eyes away from him to look around the ballroom. A few seats down on the dais the head of surgery at Memorial Hospital was listening intently. The audience was hypnotized, too; but from their expressions it was evident they didn't understand a word being said. Dr. Cambridge's fellow physicians actually looked rather awed.

Suddenly Felicity felt her heart flip over; she had a soft spot for vulnerable things, that's why she loved working with children. Quirky, handsome, monumentally self-absorbed Dr. Steven Cambridge was inciting the same sort of wobbly feelings around her heart while he read his technical dissertation to a group of people who only wanted to be entertained with a few jokes.

In the next instant Felicity gave herself a mental shake.

Stop it, she told herself, *don't go all mushy over this egotistical bonecrusher!* By now he probably hated her. An hour ago, sitting practically naked in the manager's office, he'd let her know she'd given him one of the worst evenings of his life.

She brought her attention back with an effort as Dr. Cambridge was describing anterior hemorrhaging in really gripping, pictorial terms. Two matrons at a front table struggled up from their seats and hastily left the ballroom.

Dr. Cambridge didn't notice. "And so," he said, frowning slightly as he consulted the typewritten pages of his speech, "in summary. . ."

Felicity didn't hear his last few remarks. A jittery feeling had suddenly attacked her. Now she was going to have to actually talk to him, carry on some sort of polite dinner conversation—act like a real date, even after all that had happened to them that evening. Only, she thought, biting her lip against a nervous desire to laugh, any sort of dinner conversation was out because he hadn't even had any dinner!

A spatter of polite clapping followed Dr. Cambridge back to his seat. He lowered himself into the chair next to Felicity and sat there for a moment in silence, staring straight ahead. He looked tired. He seemed to be gauging the meager applause and wondering what, if anything, had gone wrong. Finally he turned to her.

"Do you suppose I could get something to eat now?" His cobalt-blue eyes fell on Felicity, his expression—for Dr. Cambridge—fairly subdued. "I just realized I'm starv—"

At that moment Harry Tate Calloway and the Griffin Hospital director descended on them to take Dr. Cambridge away to talk to ninety-year-old Mrs. Rena McIntosh, who currently endowed the pediatric wing. Felicity watched them, noting that her date's expression was rather strange and remembering what her married women friends told her about some men being almost violent about not getting fed.

Martha Calloway quickly moved back into the empty seat beside her. "Wasn't that speech just the most *profound* thing you ever heard? I swear, I don't think there was a person in this room who understood a word of it!" She raised her voice as the orchestra struck up a dance tune. "Harry says Stevie Cambridge spends so much time in the research lab he's lost touch with reality. That boy just needs some sensible woman to take him in hand, Felicity. Give him a few tips on how to crack jokes when he makes a speech. You know, the way Harry does."

Felicity gave the banker's wife a bleak smile. Any woman who took on a tiger like Steven Cambridge was biting off more than she could chew, no matter what high hopes Martha Calloway had for *this* matchmaking venture.

Dr. Cambridge disentangled himself from Harry Calloway and the hospital director and made his way back to his seat. As he dropped down beside Felicity he looked pale.

"I wonder if you can get a hamburger in this place." He looked around for a waiter rather desperately. "Hamburger, hot dog—even a *bagel*. I haven't had anything to eat since breakfast."

No wonder he looked peaked, Felicity thought, and not just from exposure to the rain and cold. She was about to say this was the Deep South and an item like a bagel was not always the easiest thing to find on short notice, when he abruptly got to his feet.

"No wonder I feel terrible," he muttered to himself. "I'm hypoglycemic, my blood sugar levels are dropping." He pressed his fingers against the wrist of his left hand and took his pulse. "Right," he affirmed, frowning. "I need to get out of here and get something to eat."

It was Felicity's turn to pale. "Are you sick?" she whispered, getting up, too. "Is this condition, ah, chronic?"

For a long moment he looked as though he couldn't remember who she was. "Everybody gets hypoglycemic if they don't eat," he told her. "Don't make a big thing of it."

He turned away, then just as suddenly turned back, seeming to remember something. He raked fingers through thick, gold-streaked hair. "Look, if you want to stay to dance," he said almost apologetically, "I could ask a couple of the interns to come over and uh, give it a whirl."

Felicity stared at him in amazement. He had been bouncing up and down in his seat like a yo-yo, she could hardly keep track of him. Then he'd said something incoherent about blood sugar and needing to rush off somewhere to find his dinner. But "give it a whirl"? With a couple of the *interns*?

She wondered if she'd understood him correctly. He was going to pull rank, as a favor to her, and get some of the younger doctors to fill in for him? As in push his tired old blind date around the dance floor? While he called it an evening and went home to raid his refrigerator and get out of his wet clothes?

Felicity took a deep breath, her green eyes fiery. She'd really had it with Dr. Steven Cambridge!

But it was Martha Calloway who jumped into the breach. "Oh no, you can't leave," the banker's wife cried. "Not when things are just getting started! I want to see you too good-lookin' young things out there cuttin' a rug! My goodness, you're here to have a good time, remember?" She took Dr. Cambridge's hand and, with remarkable strength for someone so small, dragged him toward the dance floor.

"I really have to leave." He looked beleaguered. "I've had a heavy day and I've got to operate next week, and my schedule doesn't provide for—"

"Honey," Martha Calloway cried gaily, "don't give me that! It's not even your bedtime."

Felicity winced in spite of herself. He probably didn't deserve this; the whole dance floor was tittering. Besides, she was ready to go home; she didn't want to stay with someone who hadn't had anything to eat for sixteen hours, especially someone like Steven Cambridge and his short-term hypoglycemia. "Yes," Felicity tried to say over the loud music, "it really is time to—"

"I can't dance," Dr. Cambridge offered desperately, "I have a bad knee." He tried to demonstrate as he limped a few steps around an elderly couple doing the Lindy. "An old jogging injury, it kicks up at—"

Martha Calloway didn't buy that for a minute. "Haaa-aary," she cried. It was plainly time to appeal to a higher authority. *"Harry Tate!"*

Dr. Cambridge's reflexes were superb. Without a second's hesitation he grabbed Felicity's hand and snatched her to his hard, warm body. "Dance," he growled in her ear.

A second later they were moving to the strains of an old Rolling Stone tune, "Jumpin' Jack Flash," its original tempo considerably tamed by the Griffin Country Club orchestra.

He held Felicity in a tight grip, evidently to express the way he felt about being forced to stay there at the country club when he was pale with hunger.

Felicity tried to ignore his iron clutch, but she was close enough to hear his empty stomach rumbling. It was ridiculous, she told herself, the way some men behaved like babies about missing a meal.

They circled the dance floor in a conservative fox-trot, ignoring the couples boogieing and Lindying around them. The doctor was light on his feet and he danced beautifully. But then Dr. Cambridge, Felicity gathered, did *everything* well.

After a while, his furious grip on her was not only making people stare, it was giving Felicity a crick in her neck. She tried to pry herself away from that hard, powerful body. To be honest with herself, she admitted that dancing this close to him was a little unnerving. His virile warmth, especially the lower parts pressed against her, were making her uneasy.

But when Felicity squirmed, Dr. Cambridge only gripped her tighter. She could tell he was angry and frustrated; his fingers dug determinedly into the middle of her back to keep her still.

They foxtrotted past a table of nurses and, feeling the heat of all those openly jealous stares, Felicity tried to look unconcerned. After a few minutes she pushed Dr. Cambridge away just far enough to peer into his face. "I'm sorry," she said.

Felicity really was. There was no denying he had had a bad evening. Probably things like this—getting stuck with a blind date he didn't need or want, running over a tricycle and getting drenched in a rainstorm, having to go without his dinner—never happened to him.

But he rejected her sympathy.

"Sorry? For what?" he said stiffly. "The hospital fund dinner? My speech being a bust? Mrs. Calloway? You're hardly responsible for all that, you know."

Felicity had to admit there was some logic in that.

"Well, I'm sorry you're having such a rotten time." She tried to look up into his face, but he had her in such a convulsive grip she could hardly move.

"It's not a rotten time." Dr. Cambridge was one of the few people tall enough to look over the top of Felicity's head to some chilly point in the distance. "I'm enjoying myself immensely. After all, it isn't every week I get a chance to—what do you call it down here?" His lip curled. "Cut a rug?"

Felicity could see she'd just made a fool of herself apologizing for nothing, but her attention had wandered. She was discovering that it wasn't so much a matter of him imprisoning her in a relentless grip as it was a sort of curious, magnetic attraction.

Experimentally she tried to lean away from him. She couldn't budge. It was extraordinary. Some mysterious force held her glued to a midpoint on Dr. Cambridge's broad chest.

For a second, struggling against a power that seemed supernormal, Felicity wildly considered real magnets, odd science-fictionlike manifestations, extraterrestrial space forces and other phenomena. Then she was attacked by the dismal realization that something else was happening to them to further complicate this awful night. She knew she couldn't face it. Whatever it was.

The watered-down strains of "Jumpin' Jack Flash" beat about them as Dr. Cambridge attempted a rather complicated dip, but he couldn't move Felicity far enough away from his body to do it. He missed a beat. When he recovered, he looked at her warily. "Is something wrong?" he asked.

"My chain." Felicity's hand groping between their close-pressed bodies had just discovered the source of the mysterious magnetism. "I, ah, my chain seems to be caught on your shirt button."

"Chain?" he said, looking blank. "What chain?"

Felicity felt a sharp tug at the back of her neck where the gold chain bit into her skin. She quickly burrowed into the front of Dr. Cambridge's starchy chest to relieve the tension. The last thing she wanted was to have it break—the beautiful herringbone, solid gold chain had been a gift from her father on her sixteenth birthday.

"Will you stop doing that?" Dr. Cambridge appeared to be trying to pry her away. "Do you have some problem? Do you want to leave now?"

"We can't!" Felicity clutched him with one hand as her other worked at his shirt button surreptitiously. "The chain, my jewelry." Her voice was slightly muffled as she tried to explain. "It's tangled in your shirt." She yelped when he suddenly pulled his head back to look down. "Don't do that, you'll break it!"

Felicity threw one arm around his neck to hold him. The gesture must have looked like a burst of impetuous passion for over his shoulder she saw Martha Calloway give her the thumbs-up sign from the high table. Felicity shut her eyes.

"Would you kindly tell me what's going on?" Dr. Cambridge tugged at her impatiently. The dancers around them were regarding their struggles with interest. "And what you think you're doing?"

Felicity tightened her grip on his neck, trying to hold him still while her other hand worked furiously. "Good grief, haven't you been listening? It's my gold *chain*." She lowered her voice; she didn't want him to suddenly bolt and sever her head from her body, much as he would probably like to. "It's caught on your shirt button!"

"Button? You mean," Dr. Steven Cambridge said, making every word count, "the front of my *tuxedo*?"

He tried to draw back again to see, but Felicity clung to him frantically. "Yes, the button on the front of your tuxedo shirt. Just don't be a jerk and pull on it, okay?"

His beautiful mouth thinned as he foxtrotted through a group of second-year ophthalmology residents and their dates. "Let's get this straight," he said with deadly patience. "Something you're wearing is hung up on the front of me so we can't get apart. Is that right?"

Felicity wanted to glare at him, but she couldn't raise her head. "If you want to put it that way," she snapped, "yes!"

"I'll tell you how I want to put it," he growled in her ear. He spun her into an elaborate turn, their bodies stuck tightly together. "I want to get you out of here tonight, dead or alive, and without whatever it is you say you've got caught on the front of my shirt."

Felicity gritted her teeth. "I'm not *saying* I have anything caught on the front of your shirt," she whispered, "I have! You're tangled in my chain!"

The head of the thoracic medicine department and his wife stood back out of the way, eyebrows lifted, as Dr. Cambridge spun Felicity across the dance floor locked in their seemingly passionate embrace. "Beautiful," someone applauded from the sidelines.

Dr. Cambridge now gripped her wrist. "Will you stop it?" He managed a ghastly false smile for the crowded dance floor. "You're unbuttoning my damned shirt— you're practically undressing me here on the dance floor!"

Felicity pressed closer against him to cover what her other hand was doing. "I'm just trying to get loose," she hissed. "Why don't you stop dancing so fast? At least you could hold still a minute!"

"Are you crazy?" he hissed back. "What you're doing is *obscene!*" Seeing the reaction from the dancers around them, he smiled his terrible smile again, his stomach rumbling audibly.

"Good grief, you're paranoid, even for a doctor!" Felicity's voice rose. "Is that what you've been afraid of all evening—that I'm going to come on to you?"

People stopped dancing, fascinated. Dr. Cambridge gave them a mock-friendly wave of his hand as he whirled Felicity away. "You don't think," he growled into her hair, "that I'm ever going to forget this, do you? I ought to have my head examined for ever getting involved in this stupid—whatever it is!"

They foxtrotted rapidly through the crowded dance floor, Felicity's arm clutching his neck tightly. Out of the corner of her eye she saw Martha Calloway at the high table pointing out to Harry Tate that Dr. Cambridge was wrapped around Felicity, dancing wildly, and that Felicity was plastered against the star neurosurgeon in a very wanton manner. Things, her beaming face said, looked very promising indeed.

He was headed pell-mell for the ballroom's French doors that opened out onto the terrace. "What are you doing?" Felicity puffed, breathing hard.

"Getting you away from our audience." He released her long enough to deftly open a glass door with one hand, propelling her forward in a series of hasty, graceful steps. "So we can work on the situation."

"Wait!" Felicity screamed.

It was too late. They danced out onto the terrace into what seemed like a giant waterspout.

3

FELICITY GASPED.

There was no overhang on the country club terrace, and stepping out into the storm was like being hit with a slightly smaller version of Niagara Falls.

"My gown!" she spluttered. "I'm getting soaked!"

"Join the crowd." There was an edge of satisfaction in Dr. Cambridge's voice. "All right, let's get this over with." He put his arms around her, hands sliding to the back of her neck and the catch of the gold chain.

Even pressed tightly again him, Felicity shivered. The rain was torrential, it was insanity to stand out there; she could feel the clammy green satin of her evening gown already sticking unpleasantly to her breasts. "What's the matter with it?" she heard him mutter. "Is this the catch?" A fingernail scraped against her wet neck. "I can't open it. Why is the catch all—furry?"

"It's not fur—it's my hair." Felicity blew a rivulet of rain away from the tip of her nose. "It probably," she yelled over the torrent beating around them, "got all tangled up in the catch because you kept yanking at it."

"I didn't yank at it. I never touched the damned thing." He glared down at her, spiky dark lashes dripping water. "Well, I can't get it open, it's all furred up. You're going to have to let me go ahead and break it."

He gave an exasperated sigh. "After all, we can't stand out here all night."

Felicity recoiled, but was quickly jerked back again, the chain holding her. "No, you can't break it! It was a gift from my father!"

"Okay, then he'll have to buy you another one."

"You jerk," she cried, "my father's dead!"

Dr. Cambridge paused. In a slightly softer voice he said, "I'm sorry. But you can get it repaired."

A sob broke from Felicity that was half rage, half pain, mixed with disgust that he could make her feel that way. "You break it and I'll sue you!"

"You ought to know better than to say *sue* to a doctor." He took a deep breath. "All right, we have to do something. I'll just pull it over your head."

That was worse!

"No, you can't do—"

Too late. He slipped the chain upward. It only went halfway and jammed, hung on Felicity's ears and the thick, wet bulk of her coronet of red braids. "Ow!" she cried.

He swore, fervently. "How do I get myself into these things?" His fingers moved deftly. "Okay, just hold still while I unhook your hair."

The chain was so taut that Felicity had to slide down his wet tuxedo front and put her arms around him. Knees bent, she quivered a little against his muscular frame. Surprisingly, she felt an answering tremor from Dr. Cambridge.

In spite of the lack of room to maneuver, his agile surgeon's fingers had pulled loose Felicity's coronet of red braids. She heard him swear again, under his breath.

"Now the chain's hooked in it." He began unraveling a long plait. "Will you stop that and stand still?"

Stand still? Jammed up against him, her mouth smearing lipstick on his clammy shirtfront, she was incapable of movement. He'd started the whole thing, tangling her chain on his shirt button when he jerked her around on the dance floor. And now the idiot was tearing her hairdo apart!

In that moment Felicity hated him. Her dress was soaked, her hair was being wrecked—and she still had to go back inside and face the crowd at the country club dance!

A soggy mass fell down on Felicity's bare shoulder.

"I think," Dr. Cambridge was saying, "the chain's tangled in it a little more. But then your hair's pretty thick."

Felicity stiffened, eyes level with his collar and the bright smear of her Revlon Supergloss Rose lipstick. She didn't want to burst into angry tears; that was stupid, and they were both wet enough. She felt him brace his hard, strong length against her to get both hands free to work on the chain stuck in her hair.

Abruptly there was a pause, in spite of the storm blowing across the terrace. A strange pause, in which Felicity stopped shivering in her awkward half crouch. The moment of awareness went on as Dr. Cambridge and Felicity stood glued together in the downpour as though tightly sealed with epoxy. Where their bodies touched a strange, soggy warmth was quickly spreading. The tips of her breasts against Dr. Steven Cambridge's solar plexus were tingling and, Felicity realized, Dr. Cambridge was having a very detectable reaction, too.

"Oh, you *wouldn't!*" she cried.

Alarmed at the shimmering, burning aura of sensuality that had ignited between them, Felicity writhed. All she could think was that it was bad enough he was impossibly good-looking without being wildly sexy, too! She grabbed him when he shifted awkwardly, which pressed her mouth into his opened shirtfront and against warm skin. As her lips made contact she felt him shudder.

"Wait." He sounded oddly distracted. "I've just about got it."

But the hard bulge pressing against Felicity's front was impossible to ignore.

"You—you," she spluttered. She tried to get enough room to pull her traitorous lips away from his breastbone, her nostrils registering musky male flesh, rain, and citrusy cologne. "If you think I'm going to stand here while—"

She straightened up to eye level to glare at him.

Her gold chain broke at the same time. The end of it lashed against her chin painfully. "Ow!"

Dr. Cambridge quickly stepping back, looked defensive. "It's a reflexive action," he shouted against the rain. "It has nothing to do with you. For heaven's sake, you find it even in cadavers!"

"You're no cadaver! Oh, my chain," Felicity moaned as one of the broken halves slipped into her hand. The other hung in her hair, dangling against her cheek. "Look what you've done to me!" Hot tears mixed with the raindrops on her face. She knew she was behaving badly, but she couldn't stop. "You stupid medical moron!" she screeched.

His expression hardened. "I almost had it, and then you had to irrationally disrupt everything."

Dr. Cambridge's blue eyes were icy. If he was at all embarrassed by his body's reaction, he didn't show it. Coldly he surveyed the bedraggled sight his blind date presented—her lipstick smeared, her rain-soaked satin evening gown hanging limply, a length of wet red hair with a piece of gold chain wagging in it—and his face suddenly registered shock. He winced.

Felicity stumbled away toward the ballroom doors, but he quickly grabbed her arm. He looked pained.

"Don't make a scene about a piece of jewelry," he said hurriedly. "I'll have it repaired, I swear. I'll pay for everything. Right now I'm going to take you home. Something I should have done hours ago."

Felicity shook him off. "No, you're not! Stay here and drown, curse you!" She splashed away across the terrace. "I don't want to have to look at you another minute! Never, ever again!"

He caught up with her just as she pulled a door open.

"I *have* to take you home," he shouted over a gust of wind. "My car's at your place. And I have to call a tow truck for my Ferrari."

Felicity sagged against the door frame and shut her eyes. She'd forgotten about his sports car in her driveway. The hideous evening wasn't over, yet.

MARTHA CALLOWAY had just finished a rhumba with a young resident in pediatrics when Felicity and Dr. Steven Cambridge entered the country club ballroom.

Things had looked promising, the banker's wife thought, when Felicity Boardman and Steve Cambridge had dashed out onto the terrace and into the worst storm of the year. On second thought, though, she had her doubts about the Griffin Country Club terrace as a site for romance. What could they have been doing out there in the rain and the cold for the best part of half an hour?

Now, Martha saw, the answer was as plain as the nose on her face. Felicity's wrecked hairdo and the smear of lipstick across the young doctor's disheveled shirt certainly showed wild passion had hit them like the proverbial bolt of lightning.

Her partner was thinking something of the sort, too. "Oh, man, that's hot, that's really getting it on," the resident said, admiringly. "Underwater, yet."

They watched as Dr. Steven Cambridge, his hand at Felicity's elbow, steered his sodden companion across the dance floor and past the avid gaze of those who had seen them go out on the terrace earlier. The couple walked with eyes straight ahead, leaving a wide trail of water on the polished wood floor. The crowd drew back, out of their way.

"Hey," the young doctor murmured. "Steve Cambridge's got a real thing for tall, sexy redheads, hasn't he?"

To his surprise, Martha Calloway beamed at him. "Oh, I'm so glad you said that! She really is sexy, isn't

she? I think she's beautiful—that's what I keep telling
Harry Tate. At least everybody can see," she said, her
eyes narrowing speculatively as Felicity and Dr. Cambridge reached the outer ballroom doors, "they certainly can't keep their hands off each other!"

4

"WELL, GO ON—go *on!*" Iris's voice on the telephone reached a peak of unbearable excitement. "What happened next?"

Felicity propped her elbows on the kitchen counter, telephone receiver clamped between chin and shoulder, and stared out into the bright morning sunshine beyond her kitchen window. She supposed the story of her Saturday-night date with Dr. Steven Cambridge sounded just about as fascinating as an episode of her assistant's all-time favorite soap opera. Now that it was over, she had to admit the whole thing *did* have its uniquely dramatic elements. Not exactly Oscar-winning material, but close.

"Well," Felicity said thoughtfully, taking a sip of her coffee, "I suppose I'll never try to get in between two men to break up a fight again."

When Iris gasped, she went on, "I decided I really didn't care if they beat each other up, I was going to find a safer place. I sat down on the back steps and just watched."

On the other end of the line, Iris murmured, "Oh, wow, fantastic." The idea of two men fighting in Felicity's driveway at an early hour Sunday morning was apparently Iris's idea of the ultimate romantic experience. "Was this before or after the tow truck came for the Ferrari?"

Felicity sighed, remembering the reality.

"Iris, all this might sound very funny, but believe me, it wasn't at the time. Just think," she pointed out, "what would have happened if one of the neighbors had heard all the noise and called the police. We'd all be down at the Griffin city jail by now, trying to set bail for disturbing the peace, or assault, or something. And think of all the bad publicity for the nursery school."

Iris was unimpressed. "Walter Kendrick is such a *dork*! He's just never gotten over making all-American linebacker at Georgia Tech, he thinks it gives him a right to lean on people. I hope your hunky doctor punched him out good!"

Felicity winced. "Doctors," she reminded her, "are not natural-born prize fighters, you know."

Felicity was still tired; she hadn't slept well and the events of last night, the demon-ridden blind date, the ludicrous trouble with her gold chain that had undoubtedly made them the talk of the Griffin country club set, and then the unexpected attack on Dr. Cambridge in her driveway by little Jimmy Kendrick's father had left her exhausted.

"You mean he got hurt?" Iris had already heard from the Griffin Hospital nurses who left their children for day-care at the Gingerbread House what a hunk Dr. Steven Cambridge was. "Oh drat, Felicity, Walter banged him up? Is it bad?"

"No, no, not that, Iris. Don't jump to conclusions."

Felicity wanted to reassure her friend that he was still in one piece. But the truth of the matter was she'd been rather surprised at Dr. Cambridge's response to Walter Kendrick's early-morning assault.

Last night her neighbor'd had plenty of time to stew about little Bobby's tricycle while they were at the country club. Especially as it was still stuck under Dr. Cambridge's obviously expensive Ferrari left with its front wheels partly resting on Walter's front lawn. Right, so to speak, under Walter's nose.

The moment Dr. Cambridge brought Felicity's station wagon to a halt Walter had come charging out of his house. Before Felicity could jump from her car to stop him, an angry Walter stuck his head in the window on the driver's side, inches from Dr. Cambridge's face, and shouted accusations of reckless driving and wanton destruction of property—that is, running up on the Kendrick's grassy lawn and deliberately aiming for Bobby's tricycle.

Which was sheer nonsense, Felicity knew; Walter was just spoiling for a fight. Something about Dr. Cambridge's tall, virile frame—even in a wrinkled tuxedo—seemed to goad Walter on to rash words, insults such as "rich dude" and "weak-kneed lollipop."

When Steven Cambridge got out of his car, and even before he could get his hands up to protect himself, Walter shoved him right in the middle of his chest. He was sent reeling up against the Ferrari.

It was then a little after midnight. The neighborhood was asleep and the rain had just about stopped. The light bulb over the garage door gave enough light to see by as Walter grabbed Dr. Cambridge by the front of his jacket and slung him around. Both men went down on the ground. When they struggled to their feet, Dr. Cambridge's nose was bleeding. Felicity decided to get in between them, largely to keep Walter from damaging him any further.

From the very beginning she could see Steve Cambridge looked as though he couldn't believe what was happening. His face said this was just one more bizarre event in a truly unbelievable evening.

"You think I ran over that damned tricycle on purpose?" he managed to get out just as Walter seized him around the waist in a bear hug.

At that point things looked so bad Felicity was sure that raging, beery Walter Kendrick was going to beat Dr. Cambridge to a pulp.

"Oh, please!" she cried. "Please, not in my driveway! Can't you go somewhere else to do this?" She tried to grab Walter Kendrick's arm as he careened past with Dr. Cambridge's head under his elbow in a hammer lock. "He's a brain surgeon," she pleaded. "They need him at the hospital!"

At that exact moment, just as Felicity tried to stop Walter from using Dr. Cambridge's head as a battering ram against the garage door, he seemed to snap out of it. Stupefied, disbelieving he might have been, but he'd obviously had enough. In a move that was so quick Felicity almost didn't see it he braced himself, thrust his foot behind Walter's, then levered his body gracefully and threw Walter over his hip.

Walter Kendrick landed flat on his back in the driveway and lay there, momentarily too stunned to move.

"Don't get up," Dr. Cambridge said, dusting the front of his wrinkled tuxedo. "I have a black belt in judo. You'll only hurt yourself."

Judo, Felicity repeated silently.

With a growl, Walter got to his feet and flung himself at the other man. Dr. Cambridge promptly chopped him in the neck with the edge of his hand.

Walter staggered back, but managed to recover; he swung a roundhouse punch and connected with Dr. Cambridge's chin. With a low, irritable sound Dr. Cambridge feinted, chopped and gave Walter a sudden whack in his midsection that dropped the heavier man to the pavement to stay.

Dr. Cambridge stood over Walter, one foot on the other man's chest, looking grimly pleased with himself like some golden-haired, conquering Viking warrior. It was quite a transformation.

That was when the tow truck arrived.

"How did he look? Was he bleeding or anything?" Iris groaned. "I'd just hate it if that pig Walter broke his nose or chipped one of his teeth, or anything."

Felicity felt more than a little depressed. What had really shaken her last night was that startling purposefulness that had transformed the waterlogged figure of Griffin Hospital's star neurosurgeon into a savage, Conan-the-Barbarian-type combatant.

"Did he ask you out?" Iris went on. "I mean, did he make a date with you for next week, or something?"

"Good heavens, no." Felicity frowned. "Look, Iris, he'd just had the world's worst date, missed his dinner—he must have thought he was trapped in some sort of nightmare! Especially when he took me home and thought he was coming to the end of a miserable evening, and then Walter Kendrick came charging out at him like a crazy man." She managed a self-conscious laugh. "You don't think Dr. Steven Cambridge wants to see *me* again, do you?"

There was a thoughtful silence. Then Iris said, "Lissy, you didn't talk all last night during the dinner dance about single parenting and child deprivation and bills in Congress and stuff like that, did you?" When Felicity tried to interrupt the nursery school assistant went on relentlessly, "Because you know, you try hard to flatten a man out, I've seen you do it. Since you broke your engagement, I mean. You ruin more good dates that way."

"Oh, I *don't*," Felicity denied.

But Iris had brought up a sore subject. Secretly she had to admit that, yes, she didn't feel very comfortable on dates now, especially the blind dates her friends were always arranging for her. And maybe she *was* just a little bit hostile.

Felicity stared out at her driveway where the fight had taken place. There were still twigs and shredded leaves on the concrete by the garage doors where the two men had fallen in the bushes, and then gotten up to fight again. Something dark, not a leaf, lay in a puddle at the edge of the grass.

"Lissy, are you there?" Iris's voice said in her ear.

Felicity picked up her mug of coffee and took another sip. "I'm here," she murmured.

Was she getting warped, she wondered, getting locked into a bad attitude? After all, she wasn't the only woman in the world who'd been jilted because her fiancé had gotten another woman pregnant. And who had to call off their wedding so that he could marry his teenage lover.

There were probably others around like her, she told herself for the hundredth time; her situation couldn't be all that uncommon. Still, thinking about it made her relive the pain, the soul-grinding humiliation, all over again.

It took years for a small city in middle Georgia, where everybody knew everybody else, to forget a good story. Especially one featuring Griffin's most notable redhead—former all-Georgia center of women's southeast intramural basketball—Felicity Boardman and Michael Hanks—the best-looking man in town until Dr. Steven Cambridge had arrived, Felicity's one-time fiancé and Griffin's former high-school principal.

Michael, his teenage wife and their new baby daughter had moved to Atlanta where he was now teaching in a private school. Felicity had thought the whole sad affair would die down. But two years hadn't been enough time. Even if the town of Griffin had forgotten about it, *she* hadn't.

"I don't 'flatten' my dates," Felicity murmured. "Really, what a thing to say, Iris. When I go out with someone we—we have a good time."

"Oh, yeah? How about the argument you had with Ken Boyling at the Elks Club barbecue last July Fourth about women's sports? Getting mad and yelling that high school athletic departments don't pay to support girls's teams? That made Ken awfully mad—after all, he is head coach at Griffin High."

Felicity sighed.

"Can I help it if I feel strongly about women's sports, especially in regard to high school budgets? Do you remember how we had to practice with the worn-out basketballs left over from the boys' team?" She squinted through the glass of the kitchen window, trying to guess what that square object smack in the middle of a puddle in her driveway could be. "I should never have agreed to go to the barbecue with Ken, anyway. I probably didn't have the right attitude so soon after Michael dumped me. Besides Ken was a friend of Michael's—he probably knew Michael was running around with one of his students all the time we were engaged!"

"Ken still wanted to date you," Iris reminded her. "He asked me to call you up and see if you wanted to go with him to the barbecue, remember? He didn't ask you directly because he knew you were, ah, still coping with Michael getting married and all that."

"Ken Boyling," Felicity said bitterly, "wanted to hop into bed with Michael Hanks's ex-girlfriend, that's what he wanted. At least for the rest of the school term. It saved Ken a lot of trouble, not having to break in anybody new. And I was safe territory, not like the jailbait that ruined Michael, already bed-trained—"

"Felicity!" Iris cried, shocked. "I know Ken Boyling didn't think anything of the sort."

"Iris, you don't know a thing. In spite of what you and Martha Calloway and the whole city of Griffin might think, I'm not looking for a man. Not even a hunk like Dr. Steven Cambridge. I may be twenty-eight years old, but I'm not dying of loneliness here in my little split-level ranch-style on Alsace Drive." Felicity tried to lower her voice; there was no reason to get upset, but for some strange reason the memory of a warlike Steven Cambridge judo chopping Walter Kendrick so masterfully in the driveway last night kept popping into her mind. "Do you see me wasting away because I spend my nights at home doing my bookkeeping for the nursery school and—and watching Don Johnson on *Miami Vice*?"

She heard Iris giggle. Felicity stopped, abruptly. Good heavens, her terrible broken engagement was a matter to laugh about now?

"Really, Iris," she said with dignity, "my life didn't end when Michael Hanks played around with middle Georgia's version of a teenage Cyndi Lauper and got her in a 'delicate condition.' When I think about it, I tell myself how much they deserve each other."

"Lissy . . ." her friend began.

"Besides," Felicity said, almost to herself, "what would I do dating someone like Dr. Steven Gorgeous? We don't have a thing in common. Everybody in Griffin can tell him what a big loser I am romantically—I'm the one Michael Hanks two-timed practically up to the altar. I probably wouldn't have caught on if his girlfriend hadn't got pregnant." Felicity managed to laugh. "Besides, Dr. Cambridge is so wrapped up in his career and his ego he's already been through a bunch of broken engagements himself. For goodness sake, pity the poor women who had to put up with him, will you?"

Iris giggled again. "For someone who isn't interested in Dr. Steven Cambridge you've certainly done a lot of thinking about him. For a minute there I bought all this garbage you were giving me about him being the most awful, boring, obnoxious date you'd ever—"

"Iris," Felicity suddenly interrupted, her eyes on the curious object beyond the window glass. "There's something in my driveway. Good grief, it looks like a wallet somebody dropped last night." She needed to change the subject; the conversation about Dr. Steven Cambridge was making Felicity nervous. "Will you hold on? If it's Walter's, I'll just go up and slip it in the mailbox on his front porch while he's still sleeping." She checked her wristwatch. "It's not even nine o'clock yet. Really, I don't want to have to face Walter for the next ten years if I can help it."

Felicity laid the telephone receiver on the counter before Iris could answer and ran through the back door and out into the driveway. The puddle left behind by the night's storm was cold, and the leather wallet she fished out of it was clammy. Felicity lifted it gingerly, noting that it was a Mark Cross in expensive ostrich skin. She knew before she flipped it open that the wallet didn't belong to Walter Kendrick. He'd prefer cowhide with yellow nylon lacings and a hand-painted scene of cowboys bulldogging a steer.

"I've got Dr. Steve Cambridge's wallet," Felicity said as she slid back into her seat at the breakfast counter. "Iris, are you listening?"

As she held up the wallet a momentarily distracting picture of him wearing a pair of tightly clinging black bikini briefs in the country club manager's office suddenly filled up her mind, and she faltered.

Felicity shuddered.

Why was she having all this déjà vu, she thought desperately, these returning pictures that sent a curious thrill through her body? The man wasn't interested in her, and she wasn't going to see him again.

Good Lord, why was she thinking about Dr. Cambridge in his *underwear* at all?

"He must have dropped his wallet," Felicity muttered. "During the—well, during all that was going on last night."

Iris gave an excited squeal. "You know what that means, don't you? Oh, Lissy—you're going to have to take it back! And then he'll have to invite you out to thank you for returning it and—"

Felicity's cheeks reddened.

"I'm not going to do anything of the sort. Today's Sunday—I'll just call Dr. Cambridge's answering service and tell them I—I found it somewhere."

She found herself suddenly blushing in earnest. Of course Griffin's one telephone answering service, most of whose subscribers were the hospital's doctors, would think they knew where she'd found her date's wallet. In the back seat of her car? *Ah-hah!* Under her bed? *Ho-ho-ho!*

She swore, silently.

"I'll drop the wallet off at his office sometime to-morrow."

"You're making a mistake," Iris cried. "You're messing up! I swear, for a grown woman you do the *dumbest* things! You're going to all this trouble, calling his answering service, just so you won't have to face him in person, aren't you?"

"I've got to hang up now," Felicity said urgently. "I don't want to make a big deal of this. Let's hope he hasn't missed it yet."

She kept her fingers crossed as she dialed Dr. Steven Cambridge's office number and it rang his telephone answering service.

"Wallet?" an impersonal voice said. "You're calling about Dr. Cambridge's wallet? Um, yes."

Then voice seemed to be consulting some notes about lost wallets at length. Felicity stared out into the driveway's rain puddles as she heard the sound of pages being turned on the other end of the line, wondering why it couldn't have been Walter Kendrick's wallet she'd found. "I just wanted to leave a message," she murmured.

"Ah, here it is," the voice said. "Dr. Cambridge has already reported being robbed last night to the Griffin police. Dr. Cambridge filed a complaint this morning before he went to his cabin at the lake, and I think the police were going to go out and interview some people at the country club this morning. You're not a patient of Dr. Cambridge's, are you? If you are—"

But Felicity had frozen, telephone clasped to her ear.

"Wait—" she croaked. She was just beginning to realize what was being said, and she was horrified.

"If you're not a patient," the voice went on smoothly, "and this is in relation to the robbery, you should call Detective Capswater at the Griffin Police Department. That number is four three—"

"Lake?" Felicity almost shrieked. It couldn't be happening again, but it was! She couldn't believe it. The nightmare date hadn't ended after all! "Dr. Cambridge is at a *lake*?"

"Jodeco," the voice answered her, "Lake Jodeco. But Dr. Cambridge doesn't have a number there where he can be reached. Now, do you want me to repeat the number of Detec—"

Felicity hung up. With trembling fingers she dialed her assistant director.

Iris had been sitting right by the telephone. "What's the matter?" she demanded immediately.

Felicity didn't have time to wonder at Iris's sixth sense that something was wrong.

"Dr. Cambridge," she choked. "He's reported his wallet was stolen. To the police!"

"Well, take it right on down there. What are you waiting for? Good night, Felicity, turn it in before they come out to your house!"

But Felicity panicked. "I can't go to the police! Steven Cambridge thinks I'm responsible for everything bad that happens to him. He'll be sure I stole his wallet!"

"Oh, nonsense," Iris snorted. "Take it down to the police station. Everybody in Griffin knows where you were last night. . . . Oh," she said.

"You got it," Felicity moaned. "Everybody saw how he and I acted last night at the country club. They all think we were making out in the pouring down rain like a couple of lunatics! Then—*then* there was a fist fight right in my driveway when we got home that I hope nobody knows about! No," Felicity said, shaking her head, "what I'm going to have to do is find Dr. Steven Cambridge out at Lake Jodeco and explain the whole thing."

"Good," Iris said promptly. "I knew you were going to have to see him after all."

"Will you stop that?" Felicity cried. She grabbed up Dr. Steven Cambridge's slightly slimy leather wallet and shoved it in her shirt pocket while looking around for her car keys. "I've got to get to Lake Jodeco and find his cabin. Good grief, what does he want with a cabin, anyway?" she muttered angrily. "You'd think he'd spend all his time in an expensive condominium!"

5

IT WAS A BEAUTIFUL November day in middle Georgia,
cool and crystal clear. As Felicity drove north along the
Interstate she realized the weekend was almost gone
and she still hadn't stopped by the day-care center long
enough to take Big Bird and the Cookie Monster out of
the back of the station wagon.

That was the way her life went these days. Who
would ever think, she asked herself wearily, that running a day-care center for preschoolers would be so
hectic and all-consuming? Ever since she'd inherited the
Gingerbread House, founded by great-grandma
Mackay in 1924, Felicity had felt like the Red Queen in
Alice In Wonderland—running as hard as she could just
to stay in the same place.

The Gingerbread House's main trouble was financial. Working mothers just couldn't afford to pay what
it really took to run a day-care center. And because the
United States government had never enacted a law
providing funds for the care of children of American
working mothers the center's margin of profit, as with
all day-care operations, had always been small. In fact,
Felicity's business was a non-profit undertaking passed
on from generation to generation by the dedicated
women educators of the Mackay family.

Felicity herself had attended the Gingerbread House as a preschooler when her great Aunt Emily was the director. After college she rather reluctantly picked up the directorship when her aunt died. The tradition of running the day-care center had kept her in Griffin when at times—especially when Michael Hanks had wrecked any hope for their marriage—she might have considered moving on, perhaps to a bigger and better job somewhere else.

In the past decade, with an even larger number of women in the work force—many of them single parents—the need for day-care facilities had grown, and the Gingerbread House's money problem had worsened. Not even working as a part-time bookkeeper/accountant for a number of Griffin business firms had helped Felicity fill in the money gaps.

Even without money worries the Gingerbread House was almost too a big a job for Felicity and her two-woman staff of Iris and Cloris Jackson, who did the cooking. So many of the children needed special help. Right now their biggest problem, Felicity thought as she turned the Dodge into the Lake Jodeco Road, was "Dennis the Menace" Calhoun. And maybe four-year-old Dennis's good-looking construction worker father, who was not quite twenty-one.

Young Carl Calhoun's wife had left him to bring up Dennis alone when she went off to live with an Air Force sergeant stationed at Warner Robins Air Force Base. Marylou Calhoun had never liked being a mother—Dennis had been an "accident" that had led to both his teenage parents dropping out of Griffin High

School. Now tall, dark, broodingly good-looking Carl Calhoun was framing houses and doing general contracting work for his former father-in-law, but the strain of housekeeping and looking after Dennis was telling on both father and son. There were mornings when Carl looked suspiciously as though he were struggling with a hangover. Dennis's clothes would be soiled and looking as though he had slept in them.

Felicity, when she had time in her frantic schedule to think about it, supposed Dennis's young father needed some sort of counseling. Making more money would take care of the majority of Carl's difficulties, she knew, but that wasn't going to happen so he probably could use someone to talk to—a professional. There were crowds of young women who'd have lent him an ear, attracted to the tall, rangy figure who looked impossibly sexy in his jeans, boots and hard hat.

That included her own assistant director. Little Iris was a romantic to the core who naturally gravitated to handsome, brooding young hunks with motherless little boys. As far as Felicity was concerned Iris gave Carl too much sympathy and support.

She spotted a group of mailboxes clustered at the end of the paved Jodeco Road and slowed the Dodge. So far she hadn't seen the name Cambridge in front of any of the permanent homes. If Dr. Cambridge had what his answering service called a cabin, she guessed it was off the dirt road extension.

Years ago, Lake Jodeco had been a summer place. Now it was filled with elegant year-round residences set in shimmering, carefully manicured green lawns with boat houses and docks in back. The east end of the lake, where the asphalt road became dirt, was still untouched by developers. The shoreline was a little swampy, the road full of potholes.

Felicity couldn't help thinking, as she put the Dodge into second gear to go up a hill, that it wasn't exactly the sort of place you'd associate with someone such as brilliant, gorgeous Dr. Steven Cambridge. Griffin Hospital's young doctors and interns were usually party animals. Their specialty was houseboats and wild, late-night parties on the lake that woke up the other residents and sometimes attracted the police.

But for some reason—a desire for privacy or unsociability, perhaps—Dr. Cambridge was out here on the unfashionable part of the lake. The road came to a dead end and there was only a rutted dirt driveway straight ahead. She caught a glimpse of a log house through the bare November trees.

Felicity turned off the engine, suddenly attacked by a feeling that she was on a wild-goose chase. She didn't really need to be here, at the lake, looking for Dr. Steven Cambridge on a Sunday morning. What was it Iris had said? That if she didn't come out here to return Steven Cambridge's wallet she was missing her chance to see him again?

But she didn't *want* to see him again!

She picked her way through some tall weeds that coated her clothes with sticky beggar's lice seeds. The last thing she needed right now was to look as though she was chasing Dr. Steven Cambridge—no matter what half of Griffin thought after last night at the country club.

She knocked on the varnished pine boards of the cabin's front door. *Let's get this over with*, she thought, squaring her shoulders.

Three or four minutes later she belatedly realized no one was going to answer. However, she heard a muffled whacking, thudding sound that seemed to come from the back of the house.

She started around the side of the cabin. The odd noise might be someone chopping wood. If it was Steven Cambridge, what was she going to say to him, this man who, ever since he'd met her, had been traumatized, driven away from her presence by terrible calamities? It was almost as though they were under some ill-fated, malevolent star when they were together.

Star-crossed lovers? Felicity frowned. Why on earth had that stupid phrase popped into her mind, she asked herself. She and Dr. Cambridge were driven apart by things that kept happening. Nothing was bringing them together—that was crazy!

Still, what about the strange fight in her driveway after they'd both thought the awful evening was over? Which resulted in the lost wallet? That she had to return?

Felicity felt a little cold shiver run along her spine. When they were together she and Dr. Cambridge were a fatal combination. They brought on disasters with tricycles and Ferraris, gold chain necklaces and irascible next-door neighbors intent on assault and battery. To go any further with this—acquaintanceship—was sheer madness. She had to give him back his wallet, explain enough to make sure he didn't blame her for anything and never see him again.

Around the corner of the cabin Felicity stopped short. She saw Steven Cambridge chopping wood, taking logs from a carefully stacked crib and placing them on end to split them into firewood. He had his back to her. But what a magnificent back it was, she thought, staring.

He was naked to the waist in spite of the brisk wind that ruffled his gold-tinged hair. The way he was going at it—with methodical, violent swings of the blunt end of the ax head against a metal wedge—Felicity decided there was more involved than just a need to split firewood. Besides, the crib built into the cabin wall behind him held a head-high array of hardwood logs, enough to last for several winters.

This was obviously heavy exercise and weekend work therapy and a whole bunch of other things, Felicity supposed, as she watched the ax swing and his back muscles rippling under satiny gold skin. His broad shoulders tapered down to narrow hips, a hard, tight rear and long, muscled legs encased in well-worn jeans and heavy work boots.

He was certainly a sight, she thought, entranced. She felt a return of the curious wobbly feeling deep inside her. Supple and strong, his golden skin faintly shiny with sweat, longish hair lifting in the wind, this was the tense, arrogant neurosurgeon as she had never seen him.

"Hi," Felicity said, tremulously.

She spoke quite softly. But the effect was electric. The uplifted ax wavered, then slipped to one side and crashed into the chopping block. The untouched log fell over into the grass. Without looking up, he said in a resigned voice, "Oh, no. It can't be."

"I didn't mean to startle you," Felicity said quickly. "I pounded on your door for at least five minutes." He turned slowly to face her. "But of course no one was there to answer. . . ." Her voice trailed away.

She wondered what he was staring at. He suddenly had the most peculiar expression on his face, as though he'd never really seen her before. His gaze traveled from her feet to the top of her head.

Felicity still wore the old shirt and turtleneck sweater she'd put on first thing that morning with cotton khaki slacks, plus her Reeboks for her usual two-mile Sunday run she'd yet to take. The trip to Lake Jodeco and Dr. Steven Cambridge's cabin had eliminated that. Her hair was loose, hanging in careless disarray down over her shoulders although she had remembered to scoop part of it into a silver clip at the top of her head. The red mane flew around her face in the wind.

Dr. Cambridge couldn't seem to take his eyes off it.

"I didn't know your hair was that long," he murmured. "I didn't know women had hair that long, anymore."

It was Felicity's turn to stare. How was she supposed to respond to such a remark?

"I had it up last night, in braids," she said, frowning. It occurred to her this was the most awkward conversation she'd ever had; she couldn't understand why they were discussing her hair.

"You look like something from a fairy tale." He still held the ax in his hand, forgotten, bright blue eyes preoccupied. "It changes you completely."

"Yes, well." Felicity was uncomfortable standing there in the cold wind, but his look, his voice were mesmerizing. For a long moment they stared into each other's eyes.

"I brought your wallet back," she whispered.

"My wallet," he repeated. Her words didn't seem to be registering.

"Yes. I know you reported it stolen to the police," Felicity went on rapidly now, "but you can call them and, uh, tell them to forget it, can't you?" Finally he seemed to be paying attention, although she didn't like the look on his face; it was ominous. "You must have dropped it in the driveway during the fight with my neighbor."

The word "fight" was an unfortunate choice. Dr. Cambridge lifted the ax again and for a wild moment Felicity wondered what he was going to do. But he only bent and picked up the log and put it back on the stump again.

"Please," he said, his back to her. He swung and the ax head struck the metal wedge with a loud ringing sound. "Put the wallet down." The log split and fell in two halves at his feet. "And I'll call the police later."

She watched him bend and pick up the firewood, toss the pieces into a pile and select another log from the crib.

"You think I had something to do with this, don't you?" Felicity burst out. "Didn't I tell you? It probably dropped out of your tux when you were fighting last night!"

Crack! With a powerful swing the ax hit the wedge in the top of the new log which split in two.

He was ignoring her, very plainly telling her to leave. Well, she didn't have to have him spell it out for her. She wasn't going to stay there another moment. Felicity looked around for a place to put the wallet.

"Watch it," she heard him say.

"I'm just going to stick the wallet— Oh!" she cried.

It was almost a scream.

She'd laid the wallet on top of the stack of unsplit logs. For some reason just that small motion had set the whole six-foot-high pile to trembling visibly. Then, as the first tier of logs started to roll Steven Cambridge did what anyone would do without thinking—he stuck out both hands to hold them back. In the next instant his arms were buried in rolling hardwood.

Apparently, the shock was so intense he couldn't cry out. But Felicity saw his face go white as a sheet.

The logs continued to roll. As Felicity lunged for him, trying to help, he wrenched his arms and hands out from between the logs and stepped aside, at the same time jostling her out of the way of the falling wood.

But once set in motion the pile of logs came thundering, cascading down and kept on rolling. Some all the way across the backyard and into the trees.

"My hands," Steve Cambridge said thickly, holding them up. The skin was white where the logs had mashed them, but already there were patches of sickly red.

Felicity was horror-struck. "We've got to get you to a doctor!" At his look, she added quickly, "Another doctor, I mean."

She was feeling sick. This time it *had* been her fault. She'd been turned off by his coolness toward her, wanting to get out of there, and she'd done something incredibly clumsy putting the wallet down on top of all those precariously stacked logs. No matter how she felt about Steven Cambridge, she'd never wanted to hurt him!

She watched, alarmed, as he straightened his fingers experimentally, then clenched his hands into a fist. For a moment, seeing the look of agony on his face, Felicity thought he was going to faint.

He's braver than any man I've ever seen,, she thought, noting how tightly his teeth were clenched against the pain. But not a sound came through his lips. Many a Georgia good old boy who prided himself on how tough he was wouldn't have been able to endure what this man was enduring to test for possible fracture of his hands.

"I'll have to drive you," she told him.

The thought had occurred to him, too. He was hardly pleased. "There isn't any other way, is there?" he said.

"And ice," Felicity said helpfully. She hadn't been running a nursery school for six years without having some idea of what to do in an accident. "I'll get you a bowl and you can hold it in your lap and put your hands—"

He cut her off with a snappish, "Look, I get the idea."

For a moment Dr. Steven Cambridge looked as though his knees were going to sag and drop him to the ground. Then, with an heroic effort, he straightened up and set his shoulders stiffly. Beads of perspiration stood out on his forehead.

"Aspirin," he managed hoarsely. "I've got it in the medicine cabinet inside the cabin."

When Felicity didn't move, he looked up, blue eyes filled with pain. "What are you waiting for?" he said between clenched teeth.

She could hardly answer him. Staring at him, she knew Steven Cambridge was not only the most beautiful man she'd ever seen but the bravest. It was almost too much—it canceled out his obnoxiousness and indifference to other people's feelings and all the other things she could say about him. The important thing, Felicity realized as she stared, wide-eyed, was that she was falling in love with him.

And she had to get him to the hospital right away.

6

THE WORST PART, Felicity thought as she stood in the tiny one-room living area of the cabin several hours later, was this phone call to Iris. She preferred to believe that Felicity wanted to stay over at Dr. Cambridge's cabin on Lake Jodeco after returning his wallet for the obvious reason. It was wonderful, fantastic, Iris cried, it just proved something was still going on!

Iris didn't mind taking over the Gingerbread House all by herself, even though just coping with the usual Monday-morning chaos was really more than one person could handle. But she made it clear she wanted Felicity to forget everything and go with what she was getting into with her hunky doctor!

Felicity almost groaned out loud.

Through the window of the cabin's tiny kitchen area she could see Steve Cambridge walking restlessly up and down at the lake's edge, holding his bandaged hands up before him in a pathetic gesture of discomfort. If he held them down, the sudden rush of blood to his smashed fingers was excruciating. A bitter wind ruffled his blond hair and flattened his plaid shirt against his body. He looked rather subdued, obviously worried about the effect the accident would have on his operating schedule for the coming week.

Felicity knew he was hurting badly in spite of the pain-killing shot his friend, Dr. Greg Murphy, had given him at Emory Hospital.

She couldn't say anything to Iris about the accident because Steven Cambridge had sworn her to secrecy; it was not only his personal pride but his professional pride, too, that was involved. And seeing as this incident *was* all her fault, the least she could do, she told herself, was go along with it and help him out.

The one bright spot, she decided while listening to Iris's voice, was that she didn't have to go into another long drawn-out story explaining something that was almost too crazy to explain. Star-crossed lovers? Star-cursed lovers was more like it! She knew Steve Cambridge would be glad if he never saw her again.

That is, after the next few days.

What Felicity couldn't tell Iris was that right after the accident happened she'd raced for her station wagon, assuming they would head straight for the emergency room at Griffin Memorial Hospital.

Steven Cambridge had balked. "Not in that thing again. We'll take the Ferrari." He had hesitated, holding his hands up painfully, as though suddenly realizing his new helplessness. "Get my keys, will you? They're in my left pants pocket."

Felicity had still been shaking with shock and guilt over what had happened. "But I can't drive a Ferrari," she'd protested. "I wouldn't even know how to begin."

She'd steered him, holding a bowl of ice cubes hurriedly dragged from the cabin's refrigerator, toward the station wagon where Big Bird and the Cookie Monster regarded them through the glass of the rear window.

"Please?" she wheedled.

His face was ashen in spite of the handfuls of aspirin he'd gulped and Felicity assumed he was in too much pain to argue with her. But he could, and he did.

"We're not going to Griffin Memorial." He slid into the passenger's seat, wincing at the pain even this careful movement brought on. "Take me to Emory in Atlanta," he ordered, "I've got a friend there who'll X-ray my hands."

Felicity started the engine.

"You're not serious—all the way to Atlanta? What for? Good grief, we'd pass at least three hospitals getting there!"

He closed his eyes and leaned his head against the back of the seat.

"First," he gritted through his teeth, "I don't want the whole redneck population of Georgia to know about this stupid stunt—letting three cords of wood fall on my hands and smash hell out of them." The lines at the corners of his mouth deepened as he fought another wave of pain. "Second, I have to perform some tricky surgery week after next at the latest, the patients have been waiting for me, and I'm not going to blow it if I can help it."

Felicity had driven the car full speed down the dirt driveway.

"I don't believe you!" she'd exclaimed as they took the pot holes flying. She had only slowed when she heard his muffled expression of agony. "You think you're going to *operate* Monday? In a few days? With your hands like *that*?"

He had braced himself against the car's jolting and closed his eyes. "Just shut up," he'd growled, "and drive."

Now, with Iris going on excitedly in her ear about how Felicity needed something like this, a romantic interlude with Steven Cambridge to finally get over her busted love affair with Michael Hanks, she saw him walking up and down the lakeside, staring thoughtfully at the ground.

He looked so . . . *forlorn*, Felicity thought, surprised.

Poor Dr. Cambridge, safe for so long in his ivory research and surgery tower; he hadn't asked for all these things to happen to him. She admired him greatly for the way he'd dealt with the accident. Crushing one's hands and fingers was particularly painful, Dr. Greg Murphy had told her that in Atlanta. And not one word of blame for her. She couldn't believe it.

She couldn't understand, though, his doctor friend's reaction, and his gallows humor. After all, Steve Cambridge was his friend, wasn't he? They'd interned together. Why then had it seemed that Dr. Murphy thought the whole thing was so funny?

Dr. Murphy—the friend who was going to more-or-less secretly examine Steve Cambridge's hands and not let word get back to Griffin Memorial Hospital—had been rangy, dark and very helpful about sneaking them into Emory Hospital's deserted X-ray department that quiet Sunday. But he hadn't seemed at all sympathetic toward his old classmate. He'd seemed, on the contrary, determined to make Steve Cambridge's life miserable. Especially after he'd given Felicity a thorough, approving once-over with his roguish black eyes.

Shooting the X rays took only a few minutes, but Dr. Murphy teased Steven Cambridge relentlessly the whole time. He seemed sadistically pleased to have the rising young neurosurgeon in his power.

"You're not going to do any brain transplants with these digits, Steve-O," Dr. Murphy had chortled as he held the X-ray film of his hands up to the light screen. "Why don't you try yanking a few tonsils instead? Little kiddies are fun."

Felicity winced, looking from one to the other, not sure how to take all this. Privately, she was aghast. Dr. Murphy didn't seem to have any feeling for Steve Cambridge's suffering. And the other man took it so stoically. She knew he was in a lot of pain; the first thing Dr. Murphy had done was give him a shot. The fingers on Steve Cambridge's hands were already swelled to the size of hot dogs, and were about the same smoky red color.

"I'll operate next week," was all Steven Cambridge had said, grimly, "if it kills me."

Greg Murphy looked serious as he took down the X rays from the lighted screen.

"You know," he said to Felicity, "that's what I like about Steve. He may be a total schmooze, but don't think he won't do what he says. The guy's a killer. He drove himself like that all through medical school."

Before Felicity could open her mouth to reply Dr. Murphy's dark eyes had swept deliberately over her black turtleneck sweater and slacks just as Dr. Cambridge's had that morning. And his look stopped on her long, gleaming, now massively untidy red hair.

"Hmm, you look like you might be good for old Steve-O," Dr. Murphy said, in spite of the fact that Dr. Steven Cambridge was sitting on an examining stool right in front of them and could hear every word. "I love handsome, fascinating redheaded women," he said enthusiastically as he turned the X-ray machine off. Reaching out he touched a strand of Felicity's copper hair. "The tall, sexy kind. You know, like Snow White's wicked stepmother."

"Lay off, will you, Greg?" Dr. Cambridge said. He held both hands up in front of him to keep the blood from flowing painfully down into his fingers. "Miss Boardman doesn't understand your sense of humor."

Dr. Murphy abruptly thrust the X rays into Steven's arms.

"Steve-O needs somebody," he said, unperturbed. "He's too dedicated to science, and too young even at his age to live totally out of the world."

"Now listen, Greg—" Steven began.

But Dr. Murphy took Felicity by the arm, steering her toward the hospital elevators and leaving Steven to follow as best he could.

"The pressure bandages I put on might not help, but I like to use them. Bandages and stuff make the patients feel they're getting their money's worth."

While Felicity gaped at him, he went on, "Especially in cases like Steve's when there's not much else you can do about his hands but try to relieve the swelling."

Behind them, Steve Cambridge said, "Hell, now I wish we'd gone to Griffin Memorial. Will you cut this out, Greg?"

Dr. Murphy ignored him.

"He can't do anything with his hands in that shape," he went on. "Nothing's fractured, but there's still a lot of bruising, we don't want to minimize that. There even may be some trauma to the tendons and all that jazz. He's going to be hellishly uncomfortable." Gregory Murphy was enjoying himself. "So until he can use those hands of his you're going to have to stay pretty close, help him in and out of his clothes, feed him, take him to the potty, all that sort of thing."

Felicity stopped short in front of the elevator doors. Steven Cambridge almost ran into her.

"Feed him?" she gasped. "Do *what*?"

Dr. Gregory Murphy patted Felicity's long red hair with a gentle hand.

"Dear girl, who else?" he said, admiringly. "Steve-O wants to keep this quiet, doesn't he, until he finds out if he can operate in about ten days? Well, there you are. I know this boy. He's lacked warmth in his life, both his parents were doctors, he's never known anything not medically relevant." He pursed his lips, looking mock-judicious. "Frankly, what my colleague needs is something only you can give him, dear medieval beauty. Take him out of himself, teach him how to live again, give him a raison d'être. Lavish him with genuine, rewarding sensuousness of the most intimate and fulfilling kind. In other words," he crowed, waving his arms expansively, "TLC!"

Steven Cambridge had pushed Felicity into the elevator with his carefully upheld hands.

"Ignore this idiot," he told her. "And punch the Down button so we can get out of here."

Dr. Murphy was grinning.

"Lots of TLC, honey. Don't leave his side until he can manage to care for himself." He waved puckishly as the elevator doors began to close. "Sex is okay," he called, "there's nothing wrong with a little recreational exertion as long as you keep the hands elevated. And soak them frequently in ice packs. Name the first one," his voice floated down the elevator shaft as the cage began to move, "after me."

Felicity had been horrified. How could anybody be so callous at a time like this? And tasteless, too! She didn't understand male friendship at all. The man with her had said nothing during the elevator's descent. But as the doors opened into the hospital lobby Felicity's face had been fiery red.

She brought her attention back to Iris's voice with an effort.

"I've already been home to get my clothes," Felicity told her. "But thanks for offering to help, anyway."

In a way Felicity was vaguely irked. Her assistant obviously found it easy to believe that Felicity's sudden desire to spend a few days with this man was because they had the hots for each other. Felicity knew she'd have a hard time convincing Iris there was absolutely nothing between them. Right now he was out there walking in the wind and the cold, acting as though he couldn't bring himself back to share the cramped spaces of the cabin with her.

That, Felicity thought, looking around, was another problem. Probably the biggest problem so far.

From the looks of it the cabin had been designed for weekends. Or at most a summertime vacation. It had a bathroom and the minimal kitchen area she was standing in, and one big room with a sleeping loft above just barely big enough for a king-size bunk.

Felicity had brought along her sleeping bag, but she wasn't looking forward to curling up in front of the fireplace while Steven Cambridge took the comfortable built-in bed in the loft.

She sighed. That, unfortunately, was the way it was going to be.

The back door had been left open a crack so that he could come in without having to struggle with the doorknob with his bandaged hands. She heard his footsteps.

"I've got to go," she told Iris hastily. "Call you back later."

When she looked up, Steven was standing there, a wary expression in his blue eyes.

"What's that I smell?" he said.

He took her breath away. A gust of bracing cold air had come in with him. The tip of his nose was slightly red, but the chiseled planes of his face, his wind-tousled, gilded hair were as magnificent as ever. He held his bandaged hands before him in the unconscious attitude of a humble supplicant. If she hadn't known he was hurting pretty badly Felicity would have smiled.

"Soup," she told him. "And hot biscuits. I thought you'd be hungry. It's almost dinnertime."

He scowled. "We're out of soup."

She did smile, he looked so offended.

"Not canned soup—*homemade* soup."

"Ridiculous." The blue eyes were frosty. "I don't have anything in here to make soup with."

She turned her back on him very deliberately and began to hum under her breath. Just as deliberately, she lifted the lid on the soup pot and began to stir. Clouds of deliciously steamy homemade soup aroma floated his way.

"Oh," she murmured, "I found a carrot in the fridge. It was a little limp and moldy—" She heard him make a startled sound under his breath. "And there was an old can of tomatoes in the cabinet under the sink."

"That can of tomatoes is about three years old." He looked as though he didn't want to ask what she'd done with it. "The former owner said he put in some canned goods the last time there was an ice storm and power outage."

Felicity sighed.

"Well," she said, studying the bubbling surface of the soup, "it doesn't matter now. For the meat I had to use—"

"Don't tell me!" His voice was slightly hoarse. "I really don't want to know."

She turned around to face him, a steaming bowl of soup in her hands. His gaze went to it, reluctantly.

"I got the rest of the ingredients for my homemade soup," Felicity said sweetly, "when I stopped at the supermarket on my way back from my trip home to get my clothes."

He wasn't convinced.

"Soup," Steven said, staring at it. "Homemade soup." Then he frowned slightly and seemed to back away. "What's that green stuff floating in it?"

"Parsley!" Felicity snapped. "What's the matter with you—haven't you ever had homemade soup before?"

He lifted clear, dazzlingly blue eyes to hers. "No," he said simply, "I haven't."

7

STEVEN HELD UP a warm, golden-brown baking-powder biscuit between his bandaged hands and studied it curiously. It was his sixth buttered biscuit and his fourth brimming bowlful of homemade vegetable soup, and he'd finally satisfied his hunger enough to slow down.

"How do you make these things?" He squinted at the biscuit. "They're fantastic. I've never had anything like them before."

Felicity dropped her load of firewood on the hearth and wiped her perspiring brow with the back of her wrist. She'd concluded that if they were going to have a fire for the evening she was going to have to bring in the wood and build it herself. Because, of course, Dr. Steven Cambridge couldn't do anything with his hands wrapped in bandages.

"Martha White self-rising biscuit mix," she told him. "It's an old Southern recipe." She dropped to her knees. A curl of gray smoke twined itself rather sluggishly around the kindling, and she poked at it with a piece of wood to make it go faster.

She heard him laugh. It was a nice, surprisingly agreeable sound. She turned to look at him over her shoulder.

"It wasn't a joke," Felicity said. "Martha White biscuit mix really is an old Southern recipe."

Even as she spoke Felicity realized she would have a hard time explaining to someone like Steven Cambridge—who, after all, came from the North and whose parents had both been, apparently, self-absorbed doctors, and who claimed on top of all this that he'd never had a bowl of homemade vegetable soup—what sort of memories Martha White biscuit mix and self-rising flour would bring back. A whole generation of Southerners remembered when Martha White flour had sponsored a good part of the Grand Old Opry. And could still sing the Martha White jingle played by such country and western music immortals as Hank Williams and Roy Acuff.

Felicity watched as he tried awkwardly to maneuver the biscuit in his fingertips around his bowl to sop up the very last drop. She'd been fortunate to have her own dinner before he got started; there was hardly an inch left in the bottom of the pot.

She'd never seen anybody so ridiculously happy over a bowl of vegetable soup. What puzzled her was how anybody, even being raised in New Jersey, had lived this long without having eaten homemade soup.

"Your mother didn't cook?" she asked him.

He didn't look up. "My mother was a pathologist. She was the coroner for Temple University."

"Oh," Felicity said.

Well, she told herself as she got wearily to her feet, that explained a lot. Sometimes he acted as though he hadn't been raised among human beings. She supposed a university pathologist for a mother must have been pretty intimidating.

Felicity turned away from the fireplace and found herself staring straight into an intent, dazzling look from cobalt-blue eyes.

"I don't suppose we have dessert?" he asked, huskily.

Felicity sighed. Why did he have to look like a hopeful little boy at that moment?

"Tomorrow," she promised. "I—I make pretty good chocolate cream pie."

Darn, why had she said that? And what was this "we" business? It sounded terribly cozy.

She moved briskly toward the loft stairs. "I have to get you ready for bed," she said.

Let him make of that what he would, she told herself; they had to go to bed eventually, and she'd made up her mind she wasn't going to let herself be embarrassed again by anything. Dr. Greg Murphy in Atlanta could think the whole thing was funny if he wanted to, but right now she was worn out, bone tired from the events of the terrible day. The hurried trip home to get her clothes, making arrangements to have Iris cover for her at the nursery school, cooking dinner, hauling wood and building a fire so she could spread her sleeping bag out in front of it was all too much.

Steven stood watching her, holding his hands up in what was becoming his habitual pose. He looked preoccupied.

"Right," he said finally. He started for the bathroom door.

Felicity hauled her sleeping bag out of the kitchen area and unrolled it. A few seconds later he was back again. He looked so odd she dropped the sleeping bag and just stared at him.

"You have to help me," Steven rasped.

"Help you?" Even as she said the words she was beginning to understand. Her eyes dropped to the front of his jeans.

"Yes, my zipper," he said between his teeth. "I realize this is awkward, but you'll just have to bear with—" He stopped. Then he said harshly, "What's the matter with you?"

There were only two ways to go: embarrassment or laughter. And Felicity found to her surprise that she wasn't going to blush. For that she was grateful.

"You—you just took me by surprise."

She couldn't look at him, her lips were twitching. She was tired enough to teeter on the edge of hysterical laughter. It was unbelievable. She was going to have to help Dr. Steven Cambridge get his pants off! Just as his friend at Emory Hospital had predicted.

He was watching the ambivalent emotions play over her face.

"You don't seem to realize," Steven said stonily, "how damned difficult this all is for me. You don't think I *like* having a critical operating schedule for next week messed up, do you?" His voice was tight. "You don't think I *like* having to sneak up to Atlanta to have a smirking clown and research grant competitor like Murphy take a picture of my potentially fractured hands, do you?"

Uh-oh, Felicity told herself, *storm warnings*.

But she felt a spurt of her own redheaded anger. She gathered from the way he was talking they were just seconds away from him blaming her for the accident with the logs that had smashed his hands. *Just open your mouth*, she thought fiercely, *and chew me out. I'm surprised it hasn't come sooner.*

Felicity was startled when, instead of the tirade she expected, he abruptly turned away. The angle of his blond head, his long, graceful body, spoke of defeat and weariness.

"This is damned silly." Gilded head bowed, he studied his heavy work boots. "But I can't wait any longer," he mumbled. "Give me some help with my fly, will you?"

His change of attitude was genuine, and Felicity suddenly felt like an idiot. An insensitive one. Silly it probably was, but Steven Cambridge was not only asking for her help, he obviously didn't have any other choice!

She started toward him, but he said hurriedly, "No, not here. In the bathroom if you don't mind."

A stiff silence prevailed as Felicity followed him to the half-opened bathroom door. He leaned up against it, watching her through long lashes as she undid the cowhide Western belt that held up his jeans, then slid down the zipper of his fly. The jeans were tight. As Felicity pulled them down she uncovered the black nylon bikini briefs she remembered from the country club manager's office. Or their twin.

She tried not to look, but she couldn't help it. Steven bulged under the nylon in a totally fascinating, virile way. And standing so close to him she could feel the warmth of that glorious body and the musky smell of his skin mixed with the fresh scent of soap. She could even hear the soft, shallow murmur of his breathing. He was suddenly so enticing Felicity wanted to put her arms around him and hold him. She could hardly control herself.

"More," she heard him say huskily.

Felicity started and looked up at him, wild-eyed. Good heavens, what was he asking? His breath seemed to be coming a little more quickly. Was it possible he was feeling something similar to what she was experiencing? He certainly looked it.

He cleared his throat. "I mean," he said with an effort, "it's going to take more." He lifted his bandaged hands by way of demonstration. "The damned jeans are so tight—"

That he can't get them down over his hips, Felicity finished for him. He didn't have to complete the sentence; in that magic, breathless moment of physical closeness they seemed to be on some oddly compatible wavelength.

In the same bemused tone he said, "Please don't be upset. I don't—" He stopped, as though looking at her made him forget what he was going to say. "I don't want this to—"

"It's not bothering me." She, too, was forgetting what she was supposed to say. Dreamily she discovered her hands had somehow moved to clasp his slender hips.

She'd barely noticed. She hooked her fingers into the waistband of the jeans. "Just tell me when to stop."

"Hmm?" He was studying her halo of slightly damp red hair. "Oh, you can stop now," he told her without looking.

But it was too late.

Felicity, overcome, swayed toward him. All that lean, golden strength was exerting a mysterious power over her. Dimly she realized she would do anything he said. If he would just say it. She murmured softly, "I'll have to help you take your clothes off to go to bed, anyway."

Reality intruded with her words.

He quivered, then inhaled sharply, visibly pulling himself back from the strange spell that had held them.

"Right," Steven said. "But first things first."

Very deliberately he turned Felicity around to face the outer room.

Then he shut the bathroom door.

FELICITY SPREAD the warm down sleeping bag in front of the fireplace and quickly changed into one of her flannel nightgowns she'd brought from home. The fire burned merrily, and she knelt on the sleeping bag watching the leaping flames for what seemed like a long time.

Half an hour passed without any sign of Steven, and that stretched into almost an hour. Felicity began to be a little concerned. She had to get in there to brush her teeth and wash her face, too, she thought impatiently. She was combing out her hair with long, even strokes and yawning, when she heard sounds of a struggle. Definitely something going on in the bathroom.

She came to her feet in a rush, almost tripping on the edge of her nightgown. *Good heavens, what now?* was all she could think.

"Are you all right?" she called.

She heard a thumping sound, and then a groan.

Felicity didn't wait. She flew to the bathroom door, tried the knob and threw it open.

Steven was sitting on the only seat available wearing only his blue jeans and boots. His upper body glistened with sweat and his face was pale. He'd unwrapped and discarded his bandages. Horrified, Felicity saw his hands were dark red, streaked with blue bruising, swollen to twice their normal size. She looked quickly away.

"What have you been doing?" she demanded.

He looked grim. "I'm trying to get my boots off."

"You took your bandages off?" Her voice rose to nearly a shriek. "You're a doctor—you know better than to do something stupid like that!"

His eyes glittered. "It's because I'm a doctor," he shouted back at her, "that I knew how to get them off!"

Felicity looked down at the defiant set of his bare, powerful shoulders, the scowl on his handsome face, and realized that he really meant he didn't want her undressing him any further. It was a misguided, heroic effort to unwrap his bandaged hands; he'd apparently forgotten he couldn't slide his jeans off over his boots. Or unlace and remove his boots, either.

But he'd tried, Felicity saw, exasperated. The bumping and groaning had come, she guessed, when he tried to use the towel rack on the wall as a boot jack.

She felt ill thinking of the agony he'd put himself through. But she was beginning to have some idea of his feelings about this night they were going to spend together; he wasn't exactly comfortable with it, either.

She said more calmly, "I'll help you off with your boots."

For a moment he hesitated.

"Unless," she pointed out, "you're going to sleep in them, too."

Reluctantly, he nodded.

"I could have gotten them off," he said as Felicity straddled his leg and turned her back to him. "I was working on it."

She grabbed the heel of his work boot. "I know you were," she murmured.

Why, Felicity immediately wondered, did she want to soothe him, for goodness sake? She was treating him as if he were one of her preschoolers! But her heart did go out to him. Good grief, who would ever think Dr. Steven Cambridge would tear the bandages off his hands to try to keep a woman from undressing him?

She got one boot off, removed his thick white hunting-weight sock and started on the other.

"I'm going to have to help you with your jeans," she reminded him, puffing as she struggled to free the big work boot from his right foot. "They're too tight to get out of by yourself. Or didn't you think of that?" The boot finally came loose and Felicity lurched away, nearly hitting the opposite bathroom wall. "Now," she said, straightening up a little breathlessly, "what about getting you into some pajamas?"

He was watching her with a peculiar expression on his taut, handsome face. "I don't usually wear pajamas," he said.

Felicity found herself flushing and tried to cover it by saying, "You're going to be awfully cold tonight. Unless you want to sleep in your jeans."

"No." He was still staring at her. "I don't want to sleep in my pants. Help me out of them and I can manage the rest myself. After," he added in the same even voice, "I go up into the loft, naturally."

He stuck out his legs and with some maneuvering in the cramped space Felicity was able to pull his jeans off. She stood holding them in her hands as he stalked, straight-backed and barefooted, across the one-room cabin, naked except for his black bikini briefs, and carefully climbed the little flight of steps into the sleeping loft.

With a sigh, Felicity turned out the kitchen lights and started for her sleeping bag before the fire.

SOMETIME IN THE DARKEST HOURS of the night Felicity stirred, not quite sure what had wakened her, but aware the fire had gone out. The cabin was miserably cold.

Then she heard it. A low, mournful, less-than-human sound that made the hair on the back of her head stand up. She burrowed quickly into the soft warmth of the sleeping bag, trying to escape the noise and get back to sleep again. But it went on.

And on.

Good night! she thought, sitting bolt upright and feeling the cold immediately attack her through her night gown. What was it? Was it somebody groaning?

Groaning!

Felicity was suddenly wide awake. She scrambled out of the sleeping bag, almost tripping on the edge of her gown again as she hurried across the ice-cold floor and to the little stairs to the loft.

"I'm coming," she muttered under her breath.

The loft was almost pitch dark; it took her a moment to find the blanket-covered mound in the middle of the king-size bunk that was, apparently, Steven. It took her another moment, as she bent over him, shivering in the darkness, to realize he wasn't awake.

But he *was* moaning. The very same pain-filled noise that had made her flesh creep down below.

Wrapping her arms around her body, Felicity stared down at the man on the bed realizing he must be really hurting to groan like that in his sleep. She could hardly bear to listen to it. Was that the way he *really* felt, she wondered, all that pain? And had felt for hours, practically all day, although he stoically hadn't showed it?

"You crazy fool," she murmured softly.

Then, more practically, Felicity recalled the pain-killing shot Dr. Murphy had given him in Atlanta, which had undoubtedly worn off. She stood indecisively, biting her lip. The Emory doctor had also given her a packet of pills for pain. Maybe she should wake him up and make him take one.

Another soft groan decided her. After all, she told herself, shivering again, who could sleep with all that going on?

It took just a minute to race downstairs, find the envelope of pills Dr. Murphy had given them, draw a glass of water and run back up again. Felicity's bare feet were freezing by the time she regained the loft.

She put the glass of water down on the floor and knelt on the bed, planning to shake him awake.

He moaned again.

"Oh," Felicity moaned herself, "will you stop it?" She never could stand to see anything in pain.

"Here." She pulled the covers back, trying to find what was wrong. "Good heavens, here's the problem. You're almost sleeping on your hands. No wonder." She managed to pull them outside the blankets. They felt too heavy, puffed with swelling and they were hot. Just touching them made her realize how much they must hurt.

"What are you doing?" Steven Cambridge said thickly.

Felicity jumped. In the dark she caught the glint of light in his eyes, the outline of his golden beard-stubbled jaw.

"You were moaning in your sleep." Why did she have to sound so defensive? "I came up to see what was the matter."

"I'm sorry." He stirred restlessly and turned his head on the pillow to look at her. "Didn't mean to wake you up."

Just one look, even in the half dark, from those incredible eyes and Felicity melted. That and the fact that he was so brave about pain. And beautiful, she told herself helplessly. She had to get out of there.

"You're going to have to hold them up." She took his hands hurriedly, bent his elbows and propped them in their usual attitude of supplication. "Can you sleep with them upright like this? It's probably because they were squeezed under the c-covers—"

Inwardly Felicity groaned. Was it necessary for her to babble like this? She tried not to look at his bare, smoothly muscular chest, revealed when she'd pulled back the sheet.

"I mean, you were sleeping on them and— Here, have a pain pill," she said abruptly, shaking one out of the envelope and shoving it at him. "And wash it down with this." She bent and got the glass of water from the floor.

He did as he was told, not moving his eyes from her face as he awkwardly took the glass from her.

"Hot water bottle," he said around the pill. "I could hold it."

Felicity frowned. "Hot water bottle?"

"Yesh," he said, mouth full of water. "I could hold it. Something for my damned hands."

"Do you have one?" she wanted to know.

He shut his eyes. "No." He sighed. "Something warm. I need something hot on my hands, heat therapy. I wish I hadn't taken off the bandages."

I wish so, too, Felicity almost told him. *That's what my dad would have called a damfool stunt.* Thinking of her father brought back memories of old hunting injuries. A brilliant idea suddenly hit her.

"Hot compresses," Felicity exclaimed.

"Where are you going?" he called as she started down the loft stairs. He added, somewhat querulously, "Don't go very far, will you?"

"It's all right," Felicity called reassuringly from below. "It's only going to take a few minutes. But I'm really going to fix you up."

In the loft Steven Cambridge flinched.

8

"THIS WAS a pretty good idea." Steve examined his hands wrapped in hot kitchen towels approvingly. "I didn't know applied heat was going to help this much or I'd have asked you to do it sooner. Look—" he showed her "—I can even flex my fingers."

Stretched out beside him, Felicity was sleepy; she took his word for it. All she could see was his mitten-like hand bending slightly. If he said his fingers were flexing then that was real progress, considering all the swelling.

Felicity couldn't hold back a wide, weary yawn. It was late, she guessed, well past midnight by now.

In order to apply the hot compresses—towels taken from the kitchen and soaked in hot water—Felicity had had to climb onto the bed, wind them around his upheld hands and then hold them that way to keep them from falling off, changing the cloths every fifteen minutes or so with new ones wrung out from the pan of hot water by the bedside. It was tiring work but it made her happy to see—thanks to the pain pill, too—how much more relaxed and comfortable he was.

Felicity propped her head on her elbow and gave his right hand a check where the corner of the towel looked as though it was coming loose.

"We got the sheet damp doing this," she observed.

In the course of all the compress changing Felicity had had to take a break, stretching herself out beside him on the covers because she just couldn't sit up any longer. Now, with her hand supporting her head, lying on her side next to him, she was so close she could feel his warmth.

"It was worth it." He turned his head to look at her. "Did I say thanks? I woke you up, got you out of bed, I know you're tired."

No, she thought, as a matter of fact he hadn't thanked her for anything up until now. But this made it worth waiting for, this quiet moment when most of the tensions between them seemed to have disappeared. Felicity hadn't known they could actually be so downright peaceful together.

"Are you really sure your hands are much better?" she asked, worried. "That's awfully quick, considering you just got them smashed this morning."

"I'm using willpower, mental healing. I've got to. I can't delay operating on a three-year-old with a bad tumor." The blue eyes, cloaked with heavy black lashes, held an expression she couldn't read. "I hate fibroblastomas, the damned thing looks like a spider spread all over inside the kid's head. It will be hell getting it out."

Felicity forced her eyes open, wide.

She didn't want to drift off when he was telling her something important, something about his work; she had a feeling he rarely discussed such things with someone who was not a doctor. She was also aware that her lying in Steve Cambridge's big loft bed with part of a blanket pulled over her, propping up his towel wrapped hands and holding them was truly miraculous, considering all that had happened. She wanted, somehow, to make the most of it. Felicity also remembered a panful of water was right by the bed. She had to be careful not to step into it when she got up to leave the loft.

She didn't really want to leave, she realized. It was much warmer next to the roof. Up here, snugly under the covers, they could hear the new log she'd put on the fire crackling as it burned. The coziness made it harder to think about going back to her sleeping bag.

Felicity let her eyes close just for a moment.

"I'm betting on the willpower. Anybody who can practically ignore a pair of smashed hands all day can—" she yawned "—do anything. You're very stoic, you know. It's amazing."

She couldn't see his expression change. "Is that what you think I am—stoic?"

"Mmm." Somehow her weary head had come to rest on the pillow. "And other things."

"Like what?" he said, shifting so that he could use his thumb, carefully, to drag more of the blanket over her.

She was relaxing, *melting*, Felicity knew, against the warmth of his body. She couldn't seem to do anything about it.

"If I fall asleep," she said, her words slurred, "wake me up will you, and make me take the compresses off your hands? And the pan of water back downstairs?"

She thought she felt his light touch against her hair. She hadn't braided it back up, but had let it hang loose.

It straggled now, in a fan of disheveled sunset tangles across the pillows.

"And what other things?" he prodded her. "Besides stoic."

She really couldn't remember. The hard warmth of his body was right against hers, not even the blanket in between now. *Wake up*, Felicity's warning inner voice cried, *you can't spend the night in Dr. Steven Cambridge's bed*.

Felicity found she couldn't heed her own warning. The sleeping loft was exquisitely warm after the chilly lower part of the cabin. The enormous bed was soft, she felt as though she was sinking right into it.

"I—um," she murmured, not quite sure what they were talking about now, "I—I also think you're more sensitive than you want other people to know."

It seemed to Felicity that there was a lot of truth in what she'd just said. This was a man, after all, who worried about three-year-olds with brain tumors that he had to operate on.

"And intelligent, of course," she said with a sigh. Remembering his speech at the country club, she silently amended: make that superintelligent. Make that probably a genius. No wonder Dr. Steven Cambridge was the way he was.

He didn't seem to be listening. On one elbow now, he leaned over her, his face close to the red veil of her hair.

"What makes your hair smell like that?" he asked.

What in the world had prompted that? Felicity tried to think.

"Uh, I use a violet-scented shampoo. I think that's what it is."

Dr. Steven Cambridge's looked down at her, his beautiful azure eyes hooded, enigmatic.

"A beautiful woman," he murmured, "with long red fairy-tale hair that smells of violets."

Felicity heard those low words with a sense of shock. Had he called her beautiful? He looked absolutely serious, she thought in confusion. Not joking at all.

"I think I'd better go back down to my sleeping bag now," she said, but she didn't move.

"It's cold down there." He sat up and started pulling at the towels covering his hands. She couldn't see the expression on his face. "You'd better stay up here where it's warm." He leaned over the bed and dropped the soggy compresses into the pan of cold water and moved it away from the bed. "It's certainly big enough for the two of us."

"I don't think this is right." Felicity sat up, too. She wrapped her arms around herself and shivered. "I didn't intend to end up in bed with you." She tried to look prim. "Really."

He turned to her, bare upper body gleaming in the half-light, his swollen hands held out in front of him.

"You're safe." She thought she saw a flicker of a smile. "I can hardly molest you with these. In fact, I can't feel anything but low-level pain right now. Anything that's going to happen," he said, his voice dropping huskily, "I'm afraid you're going to have to initiate, Ms Boardman."

There followed an awkward moment. "Good grief," she whispered, mortified. She slid back down in the soft warm bed. He was right, of course. On the other hand, she wondered if he was wearing his black nylon bikini briefs. Or if he'd managed to sleep nude as he'd said.

"It *is* lovely and warm up here," she murmured, and closed her eyes.

SOMETIME IN THE NIGHT Felicity woke again, feeling heat all along her back and side that warned her she'd rolled too close to the fire. Then she remembered she was no longer downstairs in her sleeping bag in front of the fireplace. She was in Steven Cambridge's king-size bed in the loft.

The warmth, Felicity discovered groggily, was Steven Cambridge himself: his body was pressed against her, his face rested on her shoulder, he was breathing into her long tangled hair, and—good heavens!—one of his muscular, slightly hairy legs was somehow sprawled between hers. Worse, she discovered, one swollen hand lay over her breast.

In that instant, Felicity knew with a terrible clarity that it was going to be very hard to get him back on his side of the bed.

She really didn't want to. From the moment she'd laid eyes on him, tall and blond and gorgeous in his tuxedo at the back door of her house, there'd been a weird, bewitching attraction between them that made her knees weak and her heart fill with an awful yearning.

A picture of Steve Cambridge leaped into her mind as she'd seen him several hours ago, crossing the floor below on his way to the loft wearing only a pair of black nylon briefs. Trying to maintain his dignity, but vulnerable—just as he'd looked when he'd asked her if they had any dessert. Or when he'd admitted he'd never had homemade soup. Or, she thought, sighing, as he'd looked at the country club when he sat back down after his speech, realizing that almost no one had understood a word he'd said.

What a strange, quirky, brave, *beautiful* man, Felicity mused as she allowed her fingers to lightly ruffle his gold-streaked hair. She'd never met anyone quite like him. He certainly was a brilliant, complex neurosurgeon from all she'd heard; she supposed that made him unique. But he had his unguarded moments, too. He'd looked strangely wounded when Greg Murphy was teasing him unmercifully in the hospital in Atlanta.

And yes, she thought, there was something else.

She had a feeling Steven Cambridge knew how good-looking he was, but tried to ignore it. As though it made him very uncomfortable. As though it interfered, somehow, with what he wanted to be.

It wouldn't work, Felicity told herself abruptly. This man was even more difficult than Michael Hanks. And she remembered what a job *he*'d done on her ego.

Carefully she tried to slide her legs away and shift his hand off her breast. When she did, his body pressed closer to her.

"Felicity?" he murmured.

It was the first time she could remember hearing him speak her name. The queer, unexpected thrill of it made her speechless.

He dug his face even more deeply into her hair and sighed. "Violets," he said softly.

Felicity felt trapped, her heart beating wildly. All she had to do was push him away. But she couldn't! Why, she wondered crazily, couldn't they just pretend they were half asleep and make love—she was almost sure it was possible to make love like this—as though they were unconscious and didn't really know what they were doing?

He felt her trembling and went very still. He must have come wide awake, too, because he lifted himself on one elbow to look down at her.

"Felicity?" he said again.

She knew somehow he wasn't going to ask her anything. No sales talk, no persuasive line, not even wry humor.

No, that chiseled face in the half-light held an expression that was a curious mix of confident sexuality and very masculine hesitancy. *It's up to you*, his remarkable eyes said.

There was more, Felicity saw, trembling. There was heat and desire in that strong body, and tenderness, too. He wanted her. She was sure about that. For once this was no freaky accident happening to them, no weird comic scene; they were two different, strangely spellbound people there in the warm, darkened loft and the expanse of the big bed. People who could come to each other in trust, with defenses down, mistakes ignored, with no need for explanations.

Did she want him? Was that what he was asking her? Felicity was overjoyed. And scared to death!

"Yes," she breathed.

"Ah," he murmured, as though he'd just gotten what he'd wanted when he hadn't really expected to.

The first light touch of his mouth against hers was tentative, as though he was still echoing the question and her name. So close, Felicity could see thick black eyelashes like fans against his golden tanned cheekbones.

She gasped at the feather kiss, but he'd moved on to rub his lips lightly, tantalizingly, across her nose, her eyelids, a light caress for a springy curl of red hair at her temple. Felicity's body suddenly became so sensitive against the cloth of the nightgown, her breasts straining to touch his warm strength, that she could only lie trembling.

"It's all right," he murmured as he pulled aside the collar of the gown and kissed the wildly hammering pulse in her throat. "Let me."

He was so gentle—so *expert*—Felicity was stunned. But what had she expected? Dr. Steven Cambridge did nearly everything beautifully, didn't he?

But *this*! Did he know he was capturing her heart? And her soul? Would he find out she was falling desperately in love with him?

"I—I'm not very good at this," she quavered, helplessly.

"Mmm," he whispered as he nuzzled her breastbone with his warm lips.

"B-but we're c-consenting—" She could hardly speak as he unbuttoned the front of the nightgown and his mouth followed a tender trail to her breasts. "Aaaaadults," Felicity almost shrieked as his gentle kiss found her tightened, aching nipple. "Aren't we?"

She knew she should stop talking, it was not the moment for it, but she was suddenly seized with a terrible fear that they didn't know each other well enough for this. They weren't even friends!

But when he lifted his head the look in those blue eyes stopped her.

"I want to make this great for you," he said with disarming directness, "as much as I possibly can. Felicity, don't be afraid."

Inwardly she groaned. How could she resist this man when he was so wonderful?

"I'm not afraid," Felicity burst out, untruthfully. "But I'm not great at this, either. I—I just thought I'd warn you."

For a long moment he studied her, realizing there had been some other lover that had forced this confession from her.

"Ah, Felicity," he said, sighing. "I'm going to make love to you, and if you're embarrassed and hate it, it will be all my responsibility, right?"

His long, slender surgeon's hands worked the flannel gown over her head. When he had pulled it free he stopped, and stared at what he had uncovered.

"How can you be so beautiful and so damned unsure of yourself?" he murmured.

"Oh, ah," Felicity, cried, both hands moving to cover her breasts. That shimmering blue gaze burned her, like fire. "I—really..."

"Damn, I want you." There was only the barest tinge of surprise in his voice as his long body moved over hers suddenly and his fiery mouth seized hers.

As for Felicity, she was lost. The man who held her, whose mouth sent fountains of fire ripping through her as he kissed her deeply, devouringly, himself trembled with desire for her. His silky body contracted hungrily, greedily against her nakedness as caressing words tumbled into her lips. She had the most incomparably exquisite body, he muttered, the burning red hair of a fairy-tale princess, and her sensuous mouth was irresistible. He wanted her, he told her with that same odd note of muted surprise in his husky voice. She was fantastic.

The fact that Steven Cambridge could want her like that, seeking out her most intimate places, affected Felicity as nothing else had ever before. She burst into flames. *Wanton* was all she could think, dimly. Now she was the one who explored him until he shuddered. She touched him, caressed his beautiful body boldly, demandingly, as she never had with anyone.

"Ah, you're wonderful," he breathed as he maneuvered her over him, trying not to use his injured hands. "Felicity, help me." Passion made his voice hoarse. "You can do it this way, can't you?"

It was too late to tell him that no, she'd never tried to make love this way before, but as her flushed body spread open above him Felicity felt the pressure of his hot, iron-hard flesh at her most thrillingly sensitive spot. In the next breath he had pressed hard against her, pulled her onto him and entered her. With difficulty.

He was so much bigger than she expected that she gasped and cried out. Quickly his hands fumbled, painfully, to hold her to him. But she saw him shut his eyes.

"No," she told him. She knew it hurt him to hold her with his swollen hands. "Please don't."

When she moved his hands fell away.

Felicity moved again. He was so big it left her breathless and unsure and a little uncomfortable. But as she moved he came into her deeper, and deeper still, until he filled her completely. And that fanned the blaze within her body to almost painful raging. He not only possessed her, she possessed *him*, Felicity realized in a red haze of desire. It was an explosion of pure sensuality but it was more. . . .

She was looking down into the face of the man she loved. His eyes were closed, his breathing ragged, his chest heaving. He was as overwhelmed as she was, she realized dimly.

At that moment the world exploded.

Felicity went with it, convulsing and tumbling as her own response took her to a peak of flaming crying-out, giving of all she felt or could possibly feel.

Finally, after the storm, she came to rest with her cheek against his drenched skin. His heart thundered under her ear.

"No, don't move," he whispered, when she stirred. "Just stay like this for a minute."

She lifted herself enough to look down into his slightly blurry blue gaze. "Did it— Was I all right?" she murmured uncertainly. "I mean, did it—"

The blue eyes tried to focus on her.

"It was wonderful. Any better—" he tried to clear his throat "—and I couldn't stand it. Ah, Felicity, honey," he said quickly, "don't cry. What's the matter?"

"It was wonderful for me, too," Felicity said tearfully.

She slid down against him and let him hold her against his wet, still-heaving chest. *Good night, don't cry!* her inner voice admonished her. *It was fantastic and now you're going to spoil everything*.

But Felicity couldn't help it. Steven had been so tender, so passionate, so darned *great*—just as he'd said— that it was all she could do to keep from blurting out how she felt about him.

Except that she was certain he would not exactly be swept away with surprise and delight to know that she couldn't leave him, now. That she dreaded the moment when she had to go home. The time when, in fact, they had to say goodbye.

What had just happened was special, she told herself, but not anything to pin her life's hopes on. She'd learned how shaky these things could be, with Michael Hanks.

And she didn't intend to try again with someone like gorgeous, too-good-to-be-true Dr. Steven Cambridge. After all, hadn't she found out he did pretty nearly *everything* well?

"Are you sure?" he was saying. For some reason the expression on those handsome chiseled features looked untypically unsure. "Did it—was it—did it really go all right?"

"Oh yes." Felicity dried her tears with the back of her hand. What a dope she was, to go to pieces like this with the first man who'd ever made that kind of marvelous love to her! When she'd been truly responsive for the first time in her life.

She wasn't going to lay *that* on him.

Felicity lifted her head and gave Steve Cambridge what she hoped was a sophisticated, reassuring smile. "Just marvelous," she murmured, huskily.

For a moment she wondered why he looked oddly disconcerted. Or was it disappointed?

She never knew why, because he pressed her head back down against him and murmured, softly, "Let's go to sleep."

But he sighed.

9

FELICITY AWOKE to the sound of someone running around the cabin. At least that was how her sleepy brain finally identified the soft slap! thunk! that seemed to come from right beyond the log walls. She didn't need to look to know the big bed was empty.

After a while the sounds weren't so mysterious: she gathered Steve was up for early morning jogging. All that restless energy had to have some outlet, since he couldn't use his hands for chopping wood.

Smiling, Felicity straightened her body into a long, luxurious stretch against the pillows, her hands behind her head, as she thought about the night just past.

What a wonderful memory *that* was!

After they'd slept a while, wrapped around each other tightly, Steve had woken her to make love again. He'd evidently lain beside her in the dark thinking about it for a long time before he'd aroused her from her sleep with a deep, passionate kiss. He'd been so eager to make love, she thought, blushing. Wow! And with as much roaring hunger as he'd had for her Martha White biscuits and homemade vegetable soup.

Felicity had thought that particular impassioned session of lovemaking would take care of it. But just before dawn he'd wakened again with the same wonderful idea. The man was a tiger!

And a magnificent lover, she thought. She supposed it was unfair to compare Steven Cambridge with Michael Hanks, to whom she'd given her virginity and her love and her trust, only to be betrayed, but there really was no comparison.

Am I lucky or unlucky? Felicity wondered as she shrugged into her nightgown and stepped out of bed. And into the frigid pan of cold water and the soggy compresses that she'd forgotten completely.

She stared down at her bare feet in the puddles of water from the overturned pan. Perhaps this was some sort of sign, she thought, suddenly chilled with foreboding.

Were the demons that usually plagued her when she was with Steve back again after one unforgettable night of love? Felicity had known, in her heart of hearts, that such perfect bliss they'd experienced together in the night could only be temporary.

Then as if to cheer her, the heartening aroma of freshly brewed coffee drifted up to the loft. He was not only up, she thought, relieved, he'd made coffee before going outside to jog.

Felicity dressed and showered hurriedly and scooped her hair back into a long ponytail. It was Monday morning, she told herself. A glimpse at the kitchen clock showed it was eight-fifteen.

She felt disoriented as she mixed the batter for pancakes. At this hour she was usually in the midst of a noisy madhouse as mothers dropped their children off

at the Gingerbread House on their way to work. Now
here she was, in Steven Cambridge's tiny kitchen area,
fixing breakfast for the two of them.

It was impossible, though, not to worry. She just had
to find out how Iris and Cloris Jackson were coping
without her. But she knew she'd better not call them
now; she'd wait until later when the morning had settled down some and Iris could talk.

"Breakfast?" a very masculine voice said a few minutes later from the back door.

Felicity turned, her heart hammering unexpectedly.

Did he have to look so unearthly handsome just
wearing a plaid lumberjack shirt and old brown corduroy pants? There were some odd notes. For instance, his feet were stuck into sheepskin-lined
bedroom slippers and not his lace-up boots, and the
patched corduroy pants were much looser and easier
to get into than the tight blue jeans. But his golden hair
was wind ruffled, his eyes alarmingly blue, and he wore
that expectant little-boy expression that made Felicity
melt.

"Not *pancakes*?" he said almost reverently. "Real
pancakes—" He sniffed the air. "And real country sausage and real maple syrup?"

"Well, not maple syrup." She didn't know why she
was disappointed; she hadn't really expected him to
rush into the kitchen and take her into his arms and kiss
her ardently. But she couldn't keep an edge out of her
voice as she said, "It's sorghum syrup. After all, this is
the South."

After four double-sized pancakes, half a pound of country sausage patties, a large glass of freshly squeezed orange juice and two cups of coffee, Steve went outside to jog again. They hadn't talked much. But then, Felicity told herself, he had been busy eating.

Actually he'd looked so happy digging into his enormous breakfast that she'd been rather happy, too, just watching him. Then he'd decided to run all the way around the lake. He'd discovered, he'd told Felicity, that if he held his elbows tight to his body, hands braced to minimize the jolting, he could run fairly painlessly.

Felicity supposed physical activity worked off a lot of stress; hospital work—especially doctoring—was certainly the place to find more than one's share of that. She couldn't help wondering as she cleaned up the dishes what Steve Cambridge thought about as he ran around the lake road. Did he think about making love to her last night? she mused, wistfully. Because the memories were glorious.

She didn't understand why he didn't say something about it. Instead, he'd looked at her all through breakfast with those wonderful blue eyes as though trying to convey a message that she couldn't read.

Or maybe, she told herself, he really didn't have anything to say at all. Maybe last night had just been one of those things for him, another bachelor intimate encounter. After all, he *was* impossibly good-looking, women could hardly stay away from him. And as proof of that he certainly was a skilled, experienced lover. He'd been engaged . . . how many times? Four?

Feeling depressed, Felicity not only did the dishes, she also scoured the sink and cleaned out the refrigerator.

At last, when all the breakfast things were cleaned up and cleared away, she had time to call Iris, who was so busy she didn't, for once, indulge in any gleeful comments on Felicity's reasons for staying a few days at Dr. Cambridge's cabin at Lake Jodeco.

Iris, in fact, was definitely harried.

"I do *not* want you to come to Griffin, Felicity Boardman," her assistant director said loyally. "You stay right where you are. We're just missing a few extra gallons of milk, but I've called the dairy and they're going to make a special delivery out here, hopefully by lunchtime. The mumps, if that's what they are, I can take care of all by myself." When Felicity groaned out loud, she went on quickly, "I can handle it—don't get upset, will you? Last week it was a case of chicken pox, remember? I just didn't expect *three* kids to start swelling up after we had the morning cookies and fresh lemonade drinks!"

"Iris—" Felicity tried to interrupt.

But her assistant raced on, "Dennis Calhoun has had another fall, but thank goodness not here at the Gingerbread House. That kid's black and blue again. Doesn't slow him down, unfortunately. He's got more energy than ten other children his age."

Felicity frowned. "Black and blue? Doesn't that happen too often? The last time we discussed this—"

"Felicity, Dennis is just accident prone. He's a slam-bang little boy. You can't hold him still. We've hundreds of kids like him!"

Hundreds was definitely an overstatement. Four or five in as many years, maybe. And Dennis was the most rambunctious so far.

"There are warning signs, you ought to know them," Felicity cautioned. She knew how Iris felt about Dennis's good-looking father, but the Gingerbread House staff had to be alert, even with the center's usually well-parented kids, for any evidence of something more than childhood accidents.

"Carl Calhoun drinks," she added. "At least he's come in hung over a few times. And you know life hasn't been easy lately for either Dennis or his father."

"Oh, c'mon, Lissy!" her assistant cried, indignantly. "He'd never harm Dennis, he loves that child to death. Carl has a few beers once in a while, but never more than that. Why, I've never seen him—"

Iris stopped, and gave a little betraying gasp.

She'd been dating him, Felicity concluded, not all that surprised. Or at least something that passed for dating; maybe going over to his apartment or having him over to her house. She gathered Carl Calhoun didn't have enough money for many regular "dates."

A slight sound behind her made her turn.

Steve Cambridge had returned and was standing in the doorway. Felicity didn't know how much he had heard, especially her remarks about Carl Calhoun's supposed drinking, but she knew she didn't want to discuss this potential problem with anyone but Iris.

"I'll try to get in later this afternoon," Felicity said into the telephone. "I'll call you before I come."

When she hung up, he was regarding her with a thoughtful expression.

"I'm looking for something to nibble on," he said finally. "You don't make homemade cookies, do you?"

THE COLD, BRISK WEATHER turned cloudy after lunch. Steve settled himself in a battered recliner in the cabin's main room to watch an old Charlton Heston Bible epic on cable television while Felicity, still feeling disoriented because this was Monday and she wasn't at the Gingerbread House where they needed her, scrubbed the kitchen floor and then started making a chocolate cream pie.

She was still being useful. His hands weren't bandaged, but they *were* still swollen and awkward, and she knew they hurt. His frequent trips to the aspirin bottle on the kitchen windowsill showed that.

She'd handed him the soap for his shower after his run around the lake, standing discreetly behind the curtain, shaved him not too expertly, and she'd helped him on with his work boots and then tied the laces. He'd managed somehow with the zipper in the loose corduroy pants when he went to the bathroom—a delicate matter, Felicity was willing to admit, that involved masculine pride and modesty. She couldn't blame his stubborn independence on that score. But he had come to her afterward to buckle the leather belt that held them up.

There were times when she was sure he was studying her, even though he looked as though he were watching television. He snuck curious glances at her as she

GET YOUR GIFTS FROM HARLEQUIN
ABSOLUTELY FREE!

Mail this card today!

PLACE
JOKER
STICKER
HERE

PLAY THIS CARD RIGHT!

YES! Please send me my 4 Harlequin Temptation® novels
FREE along with my free Bracelet Watch and free mystery gift.
I wish to receive all the benefits of the Harlequin Reader
Service® as explained on the opposite page.

(C-H-T-10/89) 342 CIH ZDF4

NAME _____
(PLEASE PRINT)

ADDRESS _____ APT. ____

CITY _____

PROV. _____ POSTAL CODE _____

HARLEQUIN READER SERVICE®
"NO RISK" GUARANTEE

- There's no obligation to buy—and the free books remain
  yours to keep.
- You pay the low members-only price and receive books
  before they appear in stores.
- You may end your subscription anytime—just write and let
  us know or return any shipment to us at our cost.

IT'S NO JOKE!

MAIL THE POSTPAID CARD INSIDE AND
GET FREE GIFTS AND $10.60 WORTH OF
HARLEQUIN NOVELS — *FREE!*

rolled out the pie crust with a glass tumbler in place of a rolling pin.

These moments, and the deafening silence when she was buckling his belt made the tension almost unbearable. Trying to stay busy Felicity went on to fix a more elaborate meal to go with the pie than she'd intended— breast of chicken *cordon bleu* with fresh broccoli and pimento, buttered new potatoes and pecan cornbread.

At dinner there still wasn't much conversation. The strange tension persisted, although from time to time Felicity thought she caught Steve gazing at her with an almost questioning look in those dazzling blue eyes. When she glanced up, though, he looked away.

She couldn't help wondering if he was regretting last night. After all, it *was* something they really hadn't counted on, finding themselves so overwhelmingly attracted to each other, in bed together and caught up in the magic of that moment.

But Felicity decided that wasn't the problem. In fact, if there was one thing she was sure of, it was that no one could regret last night, it had been so wonderful!

She wondered if Steven was shy. She couldn't believe a man who made love so imaginatively in spite of the fact that he couldn't use his hands very well, could ever be called shy.

Well then, she decided, as she watched him help himself to more chicken *cordon bleu*, that left that Dr. Steven Cambridge, the famous neurological researcher and surgeon, perhaps not sure what subjects to talk about. Especially after what had happened between them.

If true, that really was a bad sign, Felicity thought even more desperately. It just showed there was nothing more to this—this *encounter* than just a passionate attraction. Even if the whole thing was mind-blowing. It seemed as if she was fated to be forever disappointed in love.

Felicity put down her fork.

"What's a fibroblastoma?" she asked.

He paused and looked up. "You don't really want to know about it. It's a form of brain tumor."

"Yes, I do."

Felicity found suddenly that she wanted to know anything that would help her unlock the mystery of Dr. Steven Cambridge. Her breath was fluttering nervously, just asking him.

He didn't look at her. "You're just trying to make conversation."

She shrugged. "Probably. But I'd also like to know what it is."

He shot her a look from beneath his long black lashes.

"This is probably a big mistake," Steven muttered under his breath.

He waited for her to say something, and when she didn't he said a little more loudly, "Okay, here goes."

For the next forty-five minutes Felicity sat spellbound, even forgetting the beautiful chocolate cream pie that sat waiting for them on the kitchen counter, as Steven recounted in simple terms the problems connected not only with the dread cranial fibroblastoma that, tragically, often attacked young children, but also other brain conditions that neurosurgeons encountered.

Absorbed as he was, concentrating on what he was saying, with a slight frown between those straight, dark brows, he was the most articulate, fascinating man Felicity had ever seen. What a change! She sat with both elbows on the table, not taking her eyes from his face.

"What's the matter?" he said at last. "I'm not boring you, I hope."

"Boring me?"

Hold it back, girl, Felicity told herself quickly. *Don't burst right out and tell him he's the most wonderful, brilliant man you've ever known and that you've fallen crazily in love with him. Because this is a casual thing, something that happened last night and may never happen again. He's making that clear.*

It was a moment before she could make herself say, "It didn't bore me, it was fascinating, even I could follow it. Thank you for explaining."

There was a pause.

He pushed his plate away and sat back in his chair. For a moment, puzzled, she thought he was going to say something. Then his expression changed subtly and he looked away.

"Did you say," he murmured, "something about chocolate pie?"

AS BEDTIME APPROACHED things grew even more tense. The eleven o'clock news came on and Felicity couldn't spend any more time in the kitchen cleaning up. It was already spotless.

I'm going to make a fool of myself, she thought restlessly as she looked around for something else to do and found nothing. She told herself she should go home. She could come back in the morning if he needed her. He was taking aspirin now, not powerful painkillers, so the pain must have subsided. There was nothing she could do for him during the night.

As she came into the cabin's main room he stood up to turn off the television. The silence was deep as he turned and looked at her.

"I think . . ." Felicity began, intending to tell him that she'd decided to spend the night at home.

But she never finished.

"Felicity?"

He hadn't combed his hair all day because of his injured hands. Gilded strands fell down across his forehead. The plaid shirt, the too-big corduroy pants clung to his body and accentuated its lean, muscular grace. He rendered her speechless with his vivid masculinity, his golden warmth.

Steve held out one of his swollen hands to her in appeal. He looked the way he had when she'd served him his first slice of chocolate cream pie at dinner.

"Felicity, don't sleep down here tonight," he said huskily. "Come up in the loft again. With me."

It should have been awkward, but it wasn't. Neither of them spoke as Steve moved her carefully ahead of him up the small staircase to the loft. Once they were there, the darkness and the warmth enveloped them.

He held his arms wide in a gesture of invitation. "Undress me, Felicity," he murmured.

With trembling fingers she obeyed.

It was incomparably erotic, she found, to be helping this strong, virile man out of his clothes. As she bent her head to unbuckle his belt she thought she felt the light touch of his battered fingers in her hair as though he just couldn't resist this caress in spite of the shape his hands were in. When she looked up, he smiled, his amazing eyes catching glints of the stray light from the lower room.

She thought he would say something. He took an indrawn breath, then apparently thought better of it; he only smiled again, softly.

She pulled his shirt out of the corduroy pants and slipped it down his shoulders and bare, muscular arms. When she lifted her eyes again she was mesmerized by the look on his face.

In that moment they were encompassed in a dream of tender awareness. Time was an audible, humming river that flowed hotly around them, filled with unspoken desire.

As if in a dream Felicity pulled his shirt off in slow-motion and dropped it on the floor. When she turned to the waistband of the old corduroy pants, a sharp tug revealed that he wasn't wearing any underwear. The evidence of his desire for her already stood rigid, flushed and velvety hard—magnificent.

He laughed softly at the expression on Felicity's face. "Don't look so surprised."

"That was very funny, wasn't it?" She pretended to be annoyed. " 'Felicity undress me,' " she mocked. "You knew what I'd find."

He tried to grab her by putting his forearms around her, clumsily holding his hands out of the way. "I can't do the same for you, I'm sorry. But I'd love to."

Looking into his earnest face, Felicity was suddenly inspired.

"Two can play at this game." She didn't know why, but instantly she wanted to do something wicked. It wasn't like her at all. Felicity pushed him down on the bed and straddled his legs while she pulled first his boots, then the corduroy trousers off.

Naked, he tried to sit up, but she pushed him back down again.

"So you want to help, do you?" she said with mock fierceness. "I'll show you."

She backed away while he raised himself on his elbows in the bed to watch, uncertain of what was going to happen.

Felicity gave her long mane of red hair a flip with the edge of her hand and strutted to the far end of the narrow space in the loft.

"Watch," she told him. Then she began to unbutton the buttons of her chambray shirt. Deliberately, she uncovered her best beige silk and lace brassiere filled with the curve of her slightly swaying breasts.

She almost jumped when she heard his loud groan. Then she knew he was playing along.

The groan was followed by a loud wolf whistle as she unhooked the silk scrap of a brassiere, held it between her fingers and twirled it raucously as she paced down the small space between the bed and wall again.

"Damn, I don't care if my hands are ruined," he said with a growl as she pranced by him, "I'm going to grab you."

Felicity jumped out of the way.

"Don't grab—you'll miss the best part." With a seductive shiver, she unzipped her jeans and stepped out of them.

Felicity heard a curiously strangled sound somewhere between a groan and a laugh. When she turned, her fingers hooked under the edge of the high-cut bikini panties, Steve Cambridge was watching her with an indescribable expression.

"Do you know how you look? Did you know what you just did, doing that . . . whole thing? That stripper's routine? That I'd never expect to see—" his voice shook, on the verge of laughter "—someone like you do?"

"What's someone like me?" Felicity said. She leaned over him provocatively so that the perfect globes of her white breasts swung in his face. A tight rosy nipple softly grazed his nose.

"You know what I mean," he mumbled. His mouth seized the tightened bud so hungrily that she cried out. He stroked it with his tongue until Felicity writhed helplessly.

She came down limply on the bed beside him, the mask of the stripper/seductress completely abandoned. Blindly her hands sought his thick, golden hair as his mouth devoured her breasts, making her cry out with little passionate noises.

With his mouth, because his hands were useless, he caressed her body from the sensitive inside of her palms to the silky underside of her upper arms, making her shiver. Then her breasts and her rib case, nibbling erotically.

"Let me do something for you," she moaned.

"In time." His voice was muffled as he kissed the arch of her foot, and then each toe. "I'll let you do anything to me you want."

Then, unexpectedly, he was over her in a swift, urgent movement, his big body arching as he quickly pushed her knees aside and thrust into her.

For Felicity, the sudden, explosive possession was too much. Her nerves were like over-tightened wires anyway. The abrupt thrill of his entry, the breathtaking shock of his bigness hit her. She cried out.

"Shh," he soothed her somewhat frantically. Then his lips were on hers, his body moving fierce and strong.

Felicity had never experienced anything like this. The man who held her wanted her, hungrily, overpoweringly. It was savage, erotic, ineffably tender. Their bodies were fused. Their minds. Their desires. She was dizzy with it, in complete surrender.

"Steve." She whispered his name, almost too overcome to get out the words. "I—"

She, at least, wanted to tell him how she felt. She had to; it would be dishonest to let this go any further. If she had to say she loved him, then she would.

"Don't say anything," he rasped. "Don't say—"

They began to move toward the mountain of ecstatic feeling that would sweep them away, in each other's arms, to perfect oblivion.

"Don't say anything," he managed roughly, "to spoil it."

10

FELCITY CARRIED HER BAGS out to the station wagon shortly after breakfast and threw them in the back. A bit of yellow fluff fell off Big Bird's shoulder and the papier-mâché body of the Cookie Monster shook violently, but Felicity couldn't have cared less.

She tossed in a shopping bag after her suitcase, full of spice jars, pie pan, electric skillet and all the other cooking utensils she'd brought from home. It was amazing, she fumed, how much junk she'd managed to collect in just barely two days at Steven Cambridge's Lake Jodeco cabin. And how much time and emotion she'd wasted!

He trailed her now, watching her load her things into her car, bright hair and plaid shirt flattened in the wind. He held up his hands in front of him in the old pained attitude, although Felicity knew they were much, much better. In the strained silence that had followed a stormy breakfast he'd done very well dressing himself, even slipping on his boots and managing to loosely tie the laces.

He was perfectly capable of taking care of himself. He didn't need her to look after him anymore.

Of course he'd been shocked at what had happened. He was still a little pale. But he deserved it, Felicity told herself.

It had just hit her like a bolt of lightning after a night of tender, passionate unbelievable lovemaking in his king-size bed in the loft that *this* was all there was going to be! She felt like a yo-yo. One thing at night. All business in the morning.

He'd come in after his jog around the lake looking cold, dazzlingly invigorated and happy. But all he had said to her was: "What's for breakfast?"

Somehow, for Felicity, that had torn it.

She was a mess of conflicting emotions, anyway; she'd freely admit that ever since that fatal, chaotic Saturday night at the country club she'd been slightly out of her mind. She was in love with Steve Cambridge and he didn't love her back. But she was still sane enough to know that once they'd been intimate at his cabin he'd treated her exactly like a provider of a gourmet service—great food and fantastic sex!

And there was a lot missing even from *that* basic relationship! Had he kissed her good-morning before leaving the bed? No, he was up before she was, just like the first time. Jogging around the lake. And expecting to be fed when he got back.

Had he said anything to her when he came in?

Had he taken just a minute to ask "How are you this morning?" in that particularly meaningful way that referred to all the wonderful things that had gone on between them all night?

No, Felicity had seethed as she watched him at the breakfast table chugging down his eggs and waffles and bacon and freshly squeezed juice. She knew nobody could be that crass and insensitive, no matter how brilliant he was!

Was she beginning, she raged, to feel slightly *used*? And confused about what she was doing there?

Yes!

"Fantastic," she'd heard him murmur under his breath.

It had taken a moment for Felicity to realize Steve was gazing down at his empty plate. He'd continued to study it, wind-tousled blond head bent, with such an expression of blissful satisfaction that she was stunned. Good grief, she'd thought wildly, did this handsome hunk reserve all his tenderest expressions of appreciation just for *food*? That is, any appreciation he let show.

She'd just been intimate with him! All night, practically. And she'd given him woman's greatest gift. Love!

An incredulous Felicity heard a small sound— *grrrurp!*— and realized Dr. Steven Cambridge had just belched. Contentedly.

The further realization that she was, at that moment, like a total wimp, bending over him with a pitcher of freshly squeezed orange juice to refill his glass had suddenly enraged her. She was making him even happier, she'd supposed, waiting on him. Fueling his next disgusting belch.

With a sort of crazed vengefulness Felicity had straightened up and tilted the lip of the pitcher deliberately. She let a bright, fragrant stream of orange juice flow down onto the top of Steve Cambridge's head and into his hair, dripping off his ears and into the neck of his jogging suit.

"Hey!" he'd exclaimed, jumping up. Orange juice sprayed out from his hair and the hollows in his ears as he shook his head.

Maybe it *was* a little drastic, Felicity had admitted a second later. Particularly when she hadn't said anything to him yet about why she was angry.

For a long moment he'd been dumbstruck, not looking at her, but obviously trying to adjust to what had happened. When he could finally move, he'd gone silently over to the kitchen sink and stuck his head under the faucet and turned on the cold water to get out the sticky juice.

Felicity had known, then, that Steve Cambridge had reverted to his first impression: she was simply crazy. She could tell by the way he finally lifted his eyes and looked at her, after toweling the water and juice out of his hair. But still he'd said nothing.

Now, as she got ready to leave, he merely looked resigned.

"Thank you," he was saying as she slammed the station wagon's back hatch and locked it. "I need to tell you that in spite of what you did—I mean, what happened to my hands—what you've done—" he cleared his throat "—goes way beyond a sense of duty."

Duty?

Felicity could have screamed. Didn't the man have any feelings? He still had time, if he felt anything—if he felt just one millionth of the way he did last night when he was loving her so marvelously and passionately—to say something. But blast it, he wasn't going to do it!

"I know, ah," he said, staring at her with a distant blue look, "that you have to leave. That you can't spend any more time away from work. You have to get back to the nursery."

"Child-care center," Felicity said between her teeth. "It's called the Gingerbread House and it's a facility for preschoolers."

He kept his aloof expression. "Just as you say," he murmured. "But thanks, anyway."

"Oh, forget it!" she yelled.

She was beating her head against a stone wall. He was impossible. She slammed around the side of the Dodge, yanked open the door on the driver's side and threw herself onto the seat.

Moments later she left Steven Cambridge's dirt driveway in a shower of rocks, dust and gravel and shrieking tires. She hadn't even said goodbye.

Strangely that didn't make her feel any better. Especially when she looked in the rearview mirror and saw him still standing there, a peculiarly baffled, even forlorn, look on his sculpted features.

BY TEN O'CLOCK, the Gingerbread House's early-morning mayhem had quieted and the center was well into its mostly orderly morning routine. Only Tiffany Marie Grimes looked up from the fingerpaint table as Felicity let herself into playroom B.

"We don't have any milk again," the four-year-old trilled importantly.

"Thank you, Tiffany," Felicity said, trying to look cheerful.

Actually she felt even more strangely disoriented in the familiar surroundings of the day-care center than she had at the Lake Jodeco cabin, if that was possible.

"Maybe I don't belong in this world anymore," she muttered under her breath as she went to look for Iris. "Maybe I've had an out-of-body experience and can't return to the twentieth century."

No such luck, she saw, when she found her assistant director, Iris, who was on the telephone in the kitchen. She was talking to the bookkeeping department of the Greener Pastures Dairy in Hampton.

Iris covered the mouthpiece with her hand.

"The dairy says we haven't paid the bill," she whispered to Felicity. She rolled her eyes warningly in the direction of a woman neatly attired in a blue-and-gray public health nurse's uniform who was sitting at the center's big white-painted kitchen table drinking coffee. "Myra Bates is here to look into our eight cases of mumps."

"Eight?" Felicity sent a falsely reassuring smile Myra's way. She hissed, "You told me three!"

"That was yesterday. Okay, Mrs. Josephson," Iris said quickly into the telephone receiver, "as soon as Miss Boardman comes in I'll have her call you about the bill." A second later, to be absolutely truthful, she said to Felicity, "Call Mrs. Josephson at the dairy's accounting department."

"But I paid them!" Felicity sagged against the wall as Cloris, the cook, handed her a cup of coffee. "They're wrong this time, I swear!"

Just one demand in error would wreck their cash flow this week. They couldn't pay the milk bill twice and wait for the dairy to straighten out their books—they just couldn't. She didn't have enough money in the Gingerbread House's bank account.

Iris looked sympathetic. "Welcome back from cloud nine," she murmured.

FELICITY SPENT the afternoon racing to keep up with the center's burgeoning epidemic of mumps. One by one, as Myra Grimes certified early cases, Felicity called the victims' mothers at work to tell them the bad news. She told them that they could come and pick up their children early, if they wished, and many did.

Felicity didn't have time to think. Anxious parents responded quickly and automobile traffic in the center's congested driveway by three o'clock was noisy and frantic. Children, especially the mumps victims, had to be dressed and bundled up warmly against a gray sky and a driving wind that the weather forecaster now said could become light sprinkles of snow. It took all of them working at top speed—Iris, Felicity and Cloris the cook to tend to a squirming, reluctant mass of preschoolers ready to go home. An hour or so later when the mayhem had died down Felicity wasn't even particularly happy when she located the canceled check for Greener Pastures Dairy's bill in her files.

Ten minutes spent on the telephone to the dairy's bookkeeping department wasn't very satisfying, either. The world had suddenly turned nasty and contrary for some reason. Jane Josephson at Greener Pastures, usually so accommodating and friendly, was decidedly snippy about past-due payments.

Well, Felicity had to admit, they *had* been late paying their dairy bill, not once but practically all year. But she held her ground. This time it was the dairy's fault, and she could prove it. She promised the bookkeeper she would mail her a Xerox copy of the canceled check and hung up with a sigh.

At four-fifteen she went into the rest room and washed her face and took down the tight braids that she told herself were giving her a headache.

As the red, slightly waving cloud fell around her shoulders and drifted down the back of her green sweater Felicity had a slight sense of faint, echoing, past enchantment.

Was this, she thought, peering at herself in the bathroom mirror, what she'd looked like for two of the most exquisite, unforgettable days of her life? This strange, pre-Raphaelite person, resembling a storybook illustration, really, that Steven Cambridge had likened to a fairy-tale princess?

If so, it was the first time in her life this had ever happened to her. That someone had thought nearly-six-foot-tall Felicity Boardman with freckles and a mass of ordinary red hair was desirable, attractive, and in an unguarded moment, beautiful.

Well, there was the hair, she thought, biting her lip a bit critically. It *was* just plain red. But hanging down this way...

She stopped herself short.

Come out of it, the sensible Felicity told herself. *Stop mooning at yourself in the mirror. What you're seeing may be medieval, kid, and all that jazz, but it isn't exactly dress-for-success. Where could anyone, for instance, wear almost waist-length hair except in bed? Making love?*

She sighed again. The long, red-haired woman in the bathroom mirror sighed, too.

No, it was all an illusion. She hadn't been listening carefully, that was all. Because she hadn't really been told she was beautiful. And she wasn't really in love. That was impossible.

I've done my fairy-tale princess thing, she thought philosophically, *with a truly fantastic prince. Anyone would say that much about Steve Cambridge, that he's the perfect dream Prince Charming.*

Some women never had that much, she reasoned. And maybe this was as good as it was ever going to get. She'd have her memories—Miss Felicity Boardman, the spinster child-care lady, would grow old gracefully in the small middle Georgia town of Griffin, remembering the wonderful weekend she'd spent with someone remarkable—Dr. Steven Cambridge who, alas, did not return her tender feelings.

Oh rats, she murmured under her breath.

She left her hair down when she came out of the bathroom. Iris gave her a surprised look, but for once the assistant didn't have anything to say about it. But Cloris did.

"You have to wrap your hair up if you're going to come in here," the cook told Felicity. "That's the health department what says that. And today we got Miss Myra Bates the public health nurse, too, around here."

A second later they both heard a crash and the easily identified bellow of Dennis Calhoun.

"That child," the cook grunted. "He needs a mamma to straighten him out."

When Felicity went to investigate she found Iris struggling to hold the wiry little boy in her lap.

"Leggo," Dennis was screaming.

Piles of blocks were strewn around on the playroom floor and Tiffany Marie and Jared Alan, her three-year-old brother, were screaming, too.

Another fight. Felicity sighed. Dennis liked to keep the pot boiling if nothing was going on. The way he reacted to calm persuasion was a dead giveaway, and the staff knew reasoning with him was futile. Felicity suspected his big, brooding handsome hunk of a father wasn't above giving Dennis a pop with his heavy hand once in a while. Make that pretty often, she thought grimly.

"Let me see those bruises," Felicity said, kneeling in front of Iris and the struggling child. "Dennis, hold still."

"It's nothing, Felicity." Iris looked determined. "Don't make a big thing out of it."

"How can you make a big thing out of something like this?" Felicity was tired and her temper was short; she still hadn't recovered from her scene with Steven that morning. The rest of the day had been no help, either. "Dennis will you hold *still*?"

Dennis was covered with bruises, especially his legs and arms. She held him down with her elbow while she tried to look at the parts of his grubby little body that weren't covered by his well-worn clothes. It was impossible to judge. Dennis often fought with the other children at the center. Dennis climbed to the highest heights on playground equipment, daringly. And Dennis, from what his father said, apparently was a handful at home, too.

Dennis wanted attention, she thought. He wanted his mother. And if he couldn't have her, his fear that she was gone forever made him bedevil everyone around him.

EVERY CHILD SHOULD HAVE *two parents*. Felicity could almost hear her Great Aunt Amelia Boardman, the Gingerbread House's third owner/director, saying. But times were much simpler then, back in the 1930s.

Just then the electronic bleating of the office telephone penetrated even the children's anguished screams and Dennis's furious complaints.

"I'll get it," Felicity yelled.

She raced down the hallway, threw open the office door and jerked the telephone receiver from its cradle.

It hadn't been a very good day from the moment she'd wakened to find Steve gone from the bed. And it had reached a sort of peak of horribleness when she'd given in to a very juvenile burst of temper, which she now regretted, and dumped orange juice into his hair.

Or maybe, she thought, as she lifted the receiver to her ear, this bad day had peaked at about three o'clock when all the mothers in all their automobiles had created such a traffic jam they couldn't get out of the center's driveway.

The day was winding down fast, and soon even the last of the uninfected kids would be going home. Felicity breathed a prayer for a calm finish. That nothing more would happen.

"Gingerbread House," she said a little breathlessly. "This is Felicity Boardman."

There was a most peculiar silence on the other end. But only for the briefest of seconds.

"Felicity, darling," the voice of Michael Hanks said with vast relief. "How good it is to hear your voice again, sweetheart. It's not what I usually get at home these days. Which is my kid yelling his head off, and another damned LaToya Jackson record going full blast."

11

"MICHAEL?" Felicity slumped into her office chair, her eyes glazed. "Michael Hanks?"

Her arms and legs were trembling; Michael's voice was the last thing she'd expected to hear. In fact, she couldn't believe it.

"Ah, Felicity, honey, you don't know what it's been like for me these past few months." The familiar low voice, the one that used to make her heart leap whenever he called, now spoke rapidly, as though he wanted to get as much said as possible before Felicity hung up on him.

"I know you have no reason to want to speak to me," Michael went on hurriedly, "but I've been in the pits, Felicity. Frankly I got everything I deserve. I've been doing penance on my knees the past months for being such a jerk and hurting you. Will it make you happier to know that my life's been a perfect hell since we've been apart? I've made a terrible mistake, one that I'll regret the rest of my life."

"Mistake?" Felicity croaked. "What are you talking about?"

She couldn't believe what she was hearing. Certainly Michael wasn't referring to his marriage to Griffin's former teenage sexpot? The mother of his recently born child? She was more horrified than sympathetic. Who could have any sympathy for Michael after what he had done? He'd gotten one of his students pregnant, and he'd jilted his fiancée!

There was silence on the other end of the line as though he was considering that she didn't know what he was talking about.

"Why—*us*," Michael managed in a low voice. "I'm talking about us, Felicity, and how I threw it all away. That's why I'm calling you." There was genuine regret as he said, "I want to tell you how hellishly sorry I am."

Felicity didn't know how to react to his confession. If that was what it was.

"That's all right, Michael," she said uneasily. "I don't think any apologies are necessary at this late date."

But her mind was racing. Michael Hanks was calling her to let her know that he regretted marrying his pregnant lover. She couldn't believe that, either. Did he mean that in spite of sex and passion it wasn't true love, after all? And he wished he'd stayed with Felicity? Did he want her to know that his heart was still hers, even if he'd forgotten all about it for a while? She should have been able to adjust to the strangeness, the abruptness of the message, but she couldn't.

How many times, Felicity thought suddenly, had she dreamed of this moment? To have Michael Hanks come crawling back to her, telling her what a big mistake he'd made? It ought to have been wonderful—she should have been able to gloat over it, make Michael really suffer. Instead this frantic confession wasn't at all as satisfactory as she would have thought.

Felicity sat staring into space as Michael's voice went on in her ear. She wondered if Michael meant anything to her now. It certainly didn't feel like it. Could *anyone* mean anything to her now, after the nights she'd spent in Steven Cambridge's arms? Had she let one man who didn't love her spoil her for anyone else?

Of course, she'd already worn off Michael Hanks. She reminded herself irritably that this was so much like Michael, this telephone call out of the blue, in the middle of a work day. As though her time, what she was doing, wasn't important enough to matter.

Nothing had changed.

"Michael," Felicity interrupted him, "I don't think this is very, um, proper. I mean, your calling me at work and talking to me this way. I don't think it would make your wife very happy, either, if she found out about it." She took a deep breath. "If you've got any complaints about your marriage, I suggest you take it up with her, not me."

There was a groan on the other end.

"Complaints? How can there by any complaints when a whole decade—a whole *culture* separates us? Felicity darling, I'm a baby boomer, I yearn for Rod Stewart and Olivia Newton-John—not the Fat Boys and Prince! I need someone who likes what I like. Who—"

"I can't," Felicity cried, desperately. "You're married now, Michael, you have responsibilities, just try to make something of it, will you? And please—don't call me back!"

Felicity hung up. She sat for a long moment with her head against the back of the old leather office chair, her eyes closed, telling herself she'd done the right thing.

Still, some perverse demon in her brain couldn't resist going over "what ifs." What if Michael had called before last Saturday night and her blind date? Before she'd met Steve Cambridge? How would she have reacted then? Would she have been the tiniest bit tempted to consider taking him back?

Or even more terrifyingly, the demon in her brain went on, what if Michael called in a few months? In the future when, without Steve Cambridge, she'd probably be desperately lonely and unhappy? And willing to settle for anything? Even the man who'd jilted her and wrecked her self-esteem?

Felicity moaned.

There was no way out of it, it seemed. But it was too bad she still had to live in the same town with Steve. At least Michael had had the decency to move away when he got married.

If Michael did call her again, the demon went on relentlessly, what *would* she say to him then?

Don't think about it, Felicity told herself, squelching the demon and all its horrible alternatives. *That way is madness.*

MICHAEL HANKS didn't call back, although Felicity almost expected him to. By the end of the week she had convinced herself that Michael had contacted her at a time when he was feeling low, probably for a variety of reasons. She knew that he didn't like teaching in private school, which was a comedown from the job of high-school principal. Now he was undoubtedly regretting he'd called her at all.

Steve Cambridge, though, was another matter.

Felicity couldn't help daydreaming about what she'd say to Steve Cambridge if he should just—an outside improbability, she told herself, a totally crazy idea—happen to call her someday.

He has no reason to call you, she argued with herself. *If he remembers you at all its because he misses breakfast—and a night's fantastic lovemaking!*

What happened had been a casual sexual interlude for him, a weekend of pleasantly getting it on, an incident in an eligible bachelor doctor's life. Certainly nothing major, like a meaningful love affair. Since it had meant nothing to him and she hadn't expected any better, Felicity didn't know why she was so depressed.

By the end of the week she was definitely not her usual cheerful self and everyone at the Gingerbread House had commented on it.

"Ain't no living with you these days," Cloris the cook commented with a scowl. "You runnin' short of money again, Miss Felicity? You want me to lend you some?"

"Good night, you don't make enough money to lend me any," Felicity said shortly. "Don't be foolish."

"I been playing the stock market," the big cook told her enigmatically. "What with them leveraged buyouts, I been makin' some. And stock splits and all."

"I can't cope," Felicity murmured, fleeing. "Everybody's doing better than I am!"

To Iris, Felicity gave the excuse that she was tired and that the work load at the day-care center was to blame.

Iris didn't seem to care. Some mornings Felicity would swear Iris had the warm, faintly abstracted look of a woman who's had a satisfactory night of love-making. The whole night.

"How's Carl?" Felicity asked waspishly, and hating herself. "And little Dennis?"

"Oh—okay," Iris replied, dreamily. "Dennis had the croup and Carl called me to come over, he was just out of his mind, he didn't know what those awful noises were his little boy was making. Croup *does* sound awful, you know. So I set up the vaporizer and made a croup tent, and we sat around talking until Dennis went back to sleep."

And you spent the night, Felicity added silently.

She had a sudden, searing picture in her mind of big, broodingly sexy Carl Calhoun and little cuddly blond Iris making love passionately and was astonished she could feel so envious. Lack of a sex life had never been her problem before. Or being jealous of other peoples'.

What was bothering her was certainly not Steven Cambridge, Felicity told herself. Even though she had to admit at times, especially in bed at night just before she closed her eyes, the memory of him, tall, lean and golden, came back to haunt her.

It was positively neurotic. If this kept up it would be worse than anything she'd gone through when Michael Hanks jilted her! She never imagined she'd go through the same thing a second time.

Felicity tried hard to dispel the dream. Was she really in love with him? Or had she just fallen in love with a beautiful, virile but feckless male?

Was this what happened, she thought almost hysterically, to single women of an advanced age when their full erotic nature was aroused as he'd aroused hers? Good grief—that they went clean out of their heads?

If Steve Cambridge should ever call her, make the first move, Felicity knew she'd panic. She really didn't know how to handle it. He wasn't one of the Griffin hometown boys she'd known all her life; she'd feel free to pick up the telephone if he were and start a perfectly natural, relaxed conversation.

Steven Cambridge was a tightly wound, proud, brilliant neurosurgeon; Felicity couldn't imagine a breezy, natural, relaxed conversation with him if she tried. And after all, she admitted guiltily, *she* was the one who'd walked out after that unpleasant little scene with the orange juice. Worse, she'd never explained what was the matter! She'd owed him at least that much.

MYRA BATES, the county health nurse, came back the next Monday to write a report on the total number of mumps cases the Gingerbread House had had so far that year. Myra also informed Felicity that the Griffin Health Department thought an inspection of the center's kitchen was probably in order as thirteen cases of mumps in one spot was highly suspicious. Cloris, the cook, promptly quit.

"Suspicious of *what*?" Felicity cried. "We had five cases of chicken pox this time last March and we didn't have the kitchen inspected!"

"Ain't nothing wrong with my kitchen," the cook declared as she angrily threw her extra sweater, a clean uniform and her spare shoes into a large paper bag and prepared to leave. "Nobody never accused me of having no dirty kitchen before!"

"Oh please, Cloris," Felicity cried, distracted. "Do you have to quit just before lunchtime?"

"I knows about you, too, Myra Bates," Cloris went on with ominously narrowed eyes. "You high and mighty now, Miss Public Nurse, but I used to wipe your bottom and your runny nose when you was a little gal and I worked for your mamma!"

Myra Bates turned bright red. Big, scowling Cloris Jackson was no one to have for an enemy.

"Suit yourself," the nurse said, backing down, "it wasn't my idea. The department just thought we needed to check it out."

"I check out your head, woman," the cook muttered under her breath as she went back to her work. "Don't seem to me it working right."

Myra Bates was still flushed as she went into the big assembly room to examine those of the Gingerbread House's enrollment who weren't home sick.

It was a restless crowd to have to persuade to stand still in line for any length of time. Felicity finally told those who were waiting to go back to their Lego play set on the floor, but be ready to be called.

She frowned at Iris, who was hovering in the background anxiously while the nurse looked over the children and probed the glands on their necks. When Dennis's turn came up she saw the reason for Iris's nervousness. His arms were covered with bruises and there was a big lump on his forehead.

"What's this?" the public health nurse said, turning the little boy to the light so she could see the goose egg on his forehead. "What happened to you?"

"Birds," he told her. Dennis's vocabulary was small; in spite of unlimited television viewing at home allowed by a busy father he wasn't as verbally advanced as most children his age.

"Birds did this to you?" said the public health nurse, who had heard everything. "They must have been pretty big. What kind of birds?"

"L'il," Dennis said, frowning, "L'il birds."

The county nurse looked to Felicity by way of explanation, but Iris pushed forward, instead.

"He's crazy about birds," the assistant director said nervously. "Aren't you, Dennis? Most boys like planes and spaceships, but Dennis likes birds."

She almost managed to maneuver him away from the health nurse, but Myra pulled Dennis back.

"Hold on a minute." Myra studied Dennis's arms and legs. "Have you had him worked up for possible CA?"

CA was the county's phrase for child abuse. At the sound of it, Felicity shuddered. She said a quick prayer that Iris would stay out of this.

"Dennis is our accident-prone child," Felicity began. "He has a rugged home environment, being raised by a young single parent father. But I think they're—"

"Hyperactive," Iris cried. "I swear Dennis is hyperactive! I know Dennis's father and Carl wouldn't hurt a flea. Why, he worships the ground that little boy walks on!"

Felicity swore under her breath. That's done it, she thought.

Myra Bates was a canny country girl; she looked noncommittal. "Let's have him worked up, anyway," she said, taking a notepad out of her black nurse's bag. "Just a note to his father—" she looked up for Felicity to supply the name.

"Carl Calhoun," Felicity said, unhappily.

"Ask him to bring Dennis into the Griffin Hospital clinic. If he calls, they'll give him an appointment."

Iris put both her hands to her mouth. "Oh, no," she wailed. "Don't do that."

Felicity gave her a warning look. But the damage, if you could call it that, was done. On the other hand, she thought as she watched Myra Bates write up the slip, perhaps Dennis and his father really did need to report to the clinic and get things cleared up. So far the majority of Dennis's bruises had been gotten at the Gingerbread House. Maybe all was not as suspicious as it seemed.

But Iris had fled, slamming the assembly room door behind her.

FELICITY WASN'T SURPRISED to find that Cloris, the cook, was angry with her. Even though Felicity had nothing to do with the visit from the county health department. They were all on edge. She *was* surprised, though, that Iris was angry, too.

"Now what have I done?" Felicity wanted to know.

"Nobody's here to defend Carl," the assistant director exploded. "Somebody's got to do it!"

"It isn't a question of defending Carl," Felicity said patiently. "For goodness sake, we don't even know if he's done anything, yet."

"Well, he hasn't—he *hasn't*!" her assistant cried. "It's all something cooked up by you and that damned nurse, Myra Bates!" Little Iris was quite beside herself. "It's easy to jump on Carl, isn't it? Somebody who hasn't ever had a chance in life. But then you don't have any problems, Felicity, hanging around with your rich, hunky doctor!"

"I don't know that he's rich—" Felicity began, and then stopped. She stared at Iris, who had been so supportive, who had urged her, for the most romantic of reasons, to stay at Steve Cambridge's cabin for several days. She was just beginning to realize the depth of Iris's involvement with Carl Calhoun, and she wasn't exactly pleased.

Felicity had the strange thought that none of them had had these awful problems before that fatal blind date with Steve Cambridge last Saturday night.

That was a silly idea.

"I'm not against Carl Calhoun," she told her assistant. "It's just that Dennis does stay all banged up, even for a very energetic four-year-old. Where there's smoke there's fire, Iris. It's Myra Bates's job, and I guess mine, too, to keep an eye on any situation that might indicate something's going on."

But Iris wouldn't listen to reason. "I wish you'd just leave Carl alone," she cried, tearfully.

When she left the room she slammed the door again.

Iris wasn't the only one who thought Felicity had a very ongoing relationship with Dr. Steven Cambridge. Apparently all of Griffin did, to judge from the too-casual comments and the questions about Dr. Cambridge and how he was doing these days. As though she would be the one to know. Although Felicity had to allow, a little grudgingly, that the last time anyone had seen Steve Cambridge and herself they'd been wrapped around each other in a driving rainstorm on the country club terrace!

The next week was a dreary time. The weather was bad. The mumps epidemic hadn't subsided, and the Gingerbread House was late paying more bills.

It was three weeks after her famous blind date that Martha Calloway called with an invitation to the Simon Prescotts' fund-raising dinner for the local multiple sclerosis chapter. The Prescotts—also big contributors to the neurological research clinic fund—lived in an elaborate new antebellum mansion almost as imposing as the Calloways; with swimming pool, stables and a small golf course. But the dinner dance would be held at the Griffin Country Club.

Felicity closed her eyes for a moment. She thought she knew what was coming.

How was she going to explain to Martha Calloway that Dr. Steven Cambridge was as eager to be her date again as he was to be exposed to Rocky Mountain spotted fever? It was going to take some doing. And she had to slide out of the invitation to the Prescotts' party.

"Uh," Felicity said, leaping ahead, "I think Steve Cambridge has a heavy operating schedule." Did doctors operate at night? Although it sounded strange, she'd heard some of them did. "I don't think we, ah, he'll be able to make it." Felicity hoped that sounded sufficiently unclear.

"I'm not talking about Stevie Cambridge, dear." Martha Calloway's tones were noticeably cool. "He's already responded. Stevie's bringing his former fiancée, Lyla Stamford."

"W-what?" Felicity hadn't expected that. For a moment, stupidly, she couldn't think. "What did you say?"

"Yes, dear, I hear that engagement is back on again," the banker's wife went on. "Lyla is a really beautiful girl, not too big in the brains department, but then who's to say that isn't what Steve Cambridge really needs?"

Martha Calloway paused to let that sink in. "No, for you, Felicity," she said somewhat reprovingly, "I have someone from Macon you'll love, someone more settled. His name's Augustus Prine and he's a book salesman for a very large, prestigious publisher. Is it all right if he picks you up around six-thirty?"

12

FELICITY DREADED the upcoming Saturday night. It was bad enough to be forced into another blind date, but to have to face Steven Cambridge and his on-again fiancée at the country club in front of practically the same crowd, was too much. She considered some drastic alternatives. Such as being sick. Or leaving town to visit relatives for the weekend.

Felicity rejected them all. The plain truth was she was afraid to back out.

Martha Calloway's displeasure on the telephone came across loud and clear. Steve Cambridge was back to dating his former fiancée after she, Martha Calloway, had gone to so much trouble to get Steve and Felicity together and had been so enthusiastic about the outcome—particularly after what happened in front of everybody at the hospital fund dance.

Felicity decided she'd better go along with Augustus Prine. He didn't sound too marvelous, but then, she thought gloomily, it seemed she was on everybody's hit list these days. Cloris wouldn't talk to her about the county health department's kitchen inspection, Iris thought she was persecuting Carl Calhoun, and even Dennis, who usually let Felicity rock him in the playroom big rocking chair and read *Jonathan Livingston*

Seagull to him when no one else could calm him down, acted even wilder when she was around. If a blind date was what it took to get everybody off her case, then that was what she was going to do!

Unfortunately Saturday afternoon the weather turned dark with the threat of rain.

Talk about repeat performances, Felicity thought as she got into her younger sister's slinky black velvet gown from Chicago's last winter season, all she needed was another rain storm! And Augustus Prine showing up as another irresistibly handsome, wonderful, sexy, turned-off Prince Charming. Who any normal woman couldn't understand, or get next to.

She tried to get her mind off the subject of Dr. Steven Cambridge as she worked a wide curling iron through her hair to straighten the rainy-weather curls, and piled the red mass on top of her head. Carelessly she stuck a rhinestone pin through the topknot and pulled down a few dangling curls to her neck and around her ears. Feeling even more despairing, she put on a heavy application of mauve eye shadow and black mascara and an even heavier smear of lipstick in a dark red shade she hardly ever wore.

The effect was rather curious.

Felicity squinted at herself near-sightedly in the mirror. *Wow!* she thought. Did she have the nerve to go out to the country club dressed like this—in her kid sister's almost-slashed-to-the-waist slinky black velvet that showed all the inner curves of her bare breasts? With enough high-tech makeup to qualify her for a first runner-up in a Michael Jackson look-alike contest?

She frowned. The answer was yes, she did.

She was sick of doing what everybody expected her to do, she told herself as she took her place at the kitchen window promptly at six-thirty to wait. Almost immediately an awesome silver Lincoln Continental town car whipped up the driveway and with lightning precision found the back entrance. The magnificent Lincoln pulled up inches away from a crepe myrtle tree and Felicity's rosebushes, but exactly at the overhang of the back door.

Augustus Prine leaped out. Leaped was the word, Felicity saw, her mouth open, as he almost jumped for the back porch steps and out of the steady rain. And without an umbrella.

A few seconds later, as she answered the back door, she looked into a pair of jet black eyes in a ruggedly good-looking face that featured a rakish, black, pencil-thin mustache. Her date certainly didn't look like a book salesman. With those big shoulders—even in an impeccable tuxedo—and that devilish grin, he resembled nothing more than a dashing pirate. Or Clark Gable playing Rhett Butler.

"Ah-hah," he said, looking Felicity up and down from her red topknot with its fake diamonds to the hem of her curve-clinging black velvet evening gown. "Beautiful." His voice was baritone, richly resonant. "Lady, you are truly beautiful."

Before Felicity could stop him he reached for her hand, lifted it, and pressed it to warm lips and the slightly furry feeling of the black mustache.

"*Enchanté, mademoiselle,*" Augustus Prine murmured as he kissed her fingertips. "It's going to be a great evening."

"Ah—Mr. Prine?" Felicity stammered, pulling her hand back with difficulty.

"In the flesh, beauteous one," he answered.

Good heavens, he came on strong. This date certainly was different, she'd say that. "I'm Felicity Boardman."

"Yes, I know." When Felicity reached for her old London Fog on the chair he was there before her, lifting it and whipping it around her shoulders quickly. "You don't mind a little liquid sunshine, do you?" He steered her through the back door, then took her keys from her nerveless fingers and locked it. "I got the Lincoln as close to the house as I possibly could. Here, let me lift your raincoat over your head and hold it there until we get to the car."

He smiled down at her. "Let me take care of everything, Ms Boardman," he murmured with a flash of flawlessly white teeth. "Just relax and enjoy yourself."

Dazed, Felicity realized that relaxing and letting Augustus Prine take charge was definitely the evening's program. He whisked her to his magnificent town car, holding her London Fog like a tent over her head so that not a drop of rain fell on her.

At the country club, there wasn't even a wait to get a car-park attendant—Augustus Prine flashed his piratical grin and a ten-dollar bill and they were inside and on their way to the ballroom in seconds.

Absolutely no trouble at all, Felicity thought. No smashed tricycles, no wet clothing, no exasperated, simmering partner. It was breathtaking.

And a little depressing. She sipped the champagne cocktail the book salesman brought her thinking that instead of demons attacking her evening out with Augustus Prine, the angels smiled on it. In a word, this blind date was almost perfect.

During the evening her escort charmingly danced a courtesy dance with Martha Calloway and left the banker's wife flushed with pleasure. He kept the conversational ball rolling with Harry Tate and even swapped a few raunchy jokes in his rich, booming voice. He was wonderfully attentive to Felicity, his black eyes regarding her with open admiration. But from time to time he watched her with an expression that made Felicity uneasy.

Had Martha Calloway told her date about her broken engagement with Michael Hanks? Worse, had the banker's wife told him about her recent romantic fiasco with Steven Cambridge? Felicity didn't think she could bear it if big Augustus Prine knew about her terrible social and romantic failures.

He was watching her again with that same speculative expression.

"Let's dance," Augustus Prine said, getting up and taking her hand.

The band was playing an old Beatles tune, "Michelle, Ma Belle," when they moved out onto the dance floor. Felicity stepped into the big man's encircling arms. The first thing she saw, though, when she looked over his shoulder was the golden head of Dr. Steven Cambridge not too far away in the crowd. He was dancing a fast foxtrot like the one they'd once danced together on this very floor, Felicity remembered with a sinking feeling. And in Steve Cambridge's arms was a girl just as golden and beautiful as he.

She would have to be *little*, Felicity thought with a pang. The silvery blond vision only came up to the tall doctor's black tuxedo bow tie.

Looking at her, Felicity's five-foot-ten body felt as graceful as Godzilla crushing Los Angeles skyscrapers. Instinctively Felicity slumped. And promptly stepped on Augustus Prine's foot.

"I'm sorry," she muttered.

"On the contrary." His arms circled her even more firmly, his expression inscrutable. "The body language explains everything, beautiful one. I kept getting vibrations from the moment I stepped through your back door, but frankly I couldn't put my finger on what was wrong. Now from what's just happened—you go stiff in my arms and suddenly forget how to dance, which you were doing magnificently a few seconds ago—I gather the problem is the blond dude dancing with the delectable fairy creature in blue ruffles over there."

Felicity looked at him oddly. He was right, of course, but it was uncanny.

"Did you read my mind?" she accused.

The devilish Rhett Butler grin was back.

"Actually I did. My parents were magicians—showfolks. I was born and raised in theaters, carnivals and circuses, and I can read body language as well as I can read a newspaper. Tricks of the trade. Ms Boardman, when you saw the blond gentleman across the dance floor everything came spilling out." He watched her keenly as she blushed a bright red. "Oh yes, that, too," he said softly. "Your gorgeous body told me all about it."

Felicity stopped dancing abruptly. A couple banged into them, but she didn't even notice.

Augustus Prine not only came on strong, he overstepped the bounds, she thought fretfully. True, he was a swashbuckling charmer, but Felicity was sick and tired of blind dates. Never mind Martha Calloway and the mortgage on the Gingerbread House. She didn't think she could take any more.

She started across the dance floor and the big man trailed her, looking calm.

"I'm going home," she said without turning. "You can stay if you want. I'll take a cab."

"I wouldn't think of it," he said smoothly. "But you're making a mistake to bolt and run. He won't even notice, he's busy dancing with her." He opened the outer doors of the club, and as they stepped out onto the concrete apron he signaled for his town car. "Want to go some place where we can talk?"

"Talk?" Felicity turned to him. "What have we got to talk about?"

He stared at her for a long moment. "I'll take you home," Augustus Prine said.

FELICITY HADN'T INTENDED to let him in. One evening with Augustus Prine was enough and this one had come to an end, she assured herself. But as she unlocked the back door he quickly stepped ahead of her and turned on the kitchen light.

This man took charge aggressively, she thought, annoyed. Only that good-humored self-confidence made him fairly nonthreatening.

He knew she studied him, debating whether to throw him out or not, and he cocked a black eyebrow at her. "You wouldn't offer me a cup of tea, would you?" he suggested.

"Tea?" He was full of surprises. Felicity would have expected coffee, or even a beer. "You want me to make you some *tea*?"

But he had wandered ahead of her into the living room. He stood in the center of the floor, his big-shouldered frame in the well-fitting tux, the black mustache and rakish handsomeness making him look like a figure in a magazine ad for some particularly exotic wish-fulfilling women's perfume.

"French Impressionists and wicker furniture," the book salesman murmured, his eyes lingering on Felicity's inexpensive Renoir prints over the white-painted brick fireplace. "It goes together very nicely."

Felicity relented. He was obviously enjoying the room. The tart remark about having him there uninvited died on her lips.

"I'll get the tea," she said.

"English Breakfast or Earl Grey, if you have it," his jovial baritone voice followed her as she left the room.

"NOW HERE'S WHAT I mean about body language," he said as they sat side by side on the living room couch. "The professional mind reader's unfailing tool. That is, if you do it right."

While Felicity had been making tea and cutting a few slices of Cloris's homemade butter pound cake, Augustus Prine had found the wood basket, laid a fire and lighted it. The warm blaze filled the living room with warmth and cozy, dancing light.

He took her left hand in his big ones. Felicity tried to pull back, but he held her easily.

"I don't really want my mind read," she objected.

He ignored her.

"The trick," he said smoothly, as though she weren't struggling to get her hand free, "is to maintain enough of an unencumbered grip so you can feel the subject's involuntary muscular contractions. Like, if I asked you—" his black eyes glittered "—if you were afraid of me at this moment. Ah, you see," he murmured as her fingers jumped spasmodically in his grip, "that one is very easy to read. Not panic. No, you're not the fearful type. I would say instead uneasiness with strong overtones of anger. Independent personality. You don't like being restrained. Even to learn something."

Felicity glared at him, helplessly.

"You—" She wasn't quite sure what to say. His sincerity was obvious, but in her opinion he was rather strange. That he'd been raised with carnivals and circuses gave her some idea of the kind of life he'd led. She decided she liked him, but it was hardly a romantic attraction. "Would you mind telling me what you're getting at?" she said with asperity.

He studied her, too, for a long moment. Oddly, he appeared to struggle with some emotion. His expression might have been that of someone relinquishing a dream.

"It is not to be," he said at last, softly. "Although when I first saw you I said to myself, this is the one, Gus—the fairy-tale princess they say you're destined to find. You certainly looked the part, Ms Boardman, with diamonds in that wonderful hair and that witch's black velvet gown."

His voice deepened as he shifted his body closer to her.

"I told you I was born into carnivals and circus life, didn't I? My parents had a mind-reading act, a pretty good one at times when my dad was sober. My mother—" His black eyes looked faraway for the briefest of moments. "My mother was a beautiful doll, bless her. She kept things together even when they were on stage and my father was too blasted to remember his cues. But my mother wore wonderful costumes, all glitter and white spangles, and she was so lovely half the time the audience didn't know when my old man blew his mind-reading part. Anyway," he said abruptly, "there were a bunch of gypsies in one particular circus we were traveling with, and they told my fortune for real—or so they said. They bragged it was none of the stagey fake stuff my parents were doing. The grandmother, the old gypsy queen latched on to me. She said my fortune was so interesting she had to do it. For free."

"Really, I—" Felicity murmured, tugging at her hand. But he held it fast, not releasing her.

"Know what she told me?" He seemed deep in his memories. "I was only sixteen and it made a hell of an impression on me. The old girl took me in with her gypsy scam—me, a wise carny boy! Scared the lights out of me, but I believed her when she said I was going to meet a beautiful princess-type locked away from the world. 'Her own jailer.' Curious words, right?—living under a spell that I would break. And find true happiness after all these years." His black eyes fixed reminiscently at a spot over her head. "After all these years," he almost whispered, "of wandering."

Felicity felt a slight chill.

She wasn't exactly afraid of Augustus Prine, but he did have an oddly supernormal air about him at times that was curiously convincing, given his handsome, piratical exterior.

"However," he went on, "I see your fate, lovely Ms Boardman, is intertwined with the young Lancelot we saw at the dance and not a reformed ex-circus wizard like me. Too bad."

Felicity jerked her hand in his grasp.

"I don't know what you're talking about." He was much too perceptive. Augustus Prine didn't have the right to know that much about her. And she'd had enough of weird gypsy forecasting about princesses that needed rescuing. "Please, let go of my hand!"

But those black, penetrating eyes were right in hers. He did not release her.

"It's not magic," he assured her, "don't look so scared. You're reacting to what I'm saying. Remember, dear lady, the subject was body language." Augustus Prine paused, significantly. "It tells the truth even when you don't. At one time I made a decent living this way. Holding people's hands and doing a mind-reading act. But it was their hands' muscle spasms I read, not their minds."

Inwardly Felicity groaned. This was not the way she'd expected the evening to end. With this all-too-clever book salesman lecturing her on bizarre subjects like mind reading and gypsy fortune-telling.

"Look, I don't deserve this." She looked straight at him. "I'm swearing off blind dates, do you hear me? I'll never go on another one again!"

He didn't smile.

"I gather," he said judiciously, "that he doesn't know you're in love with him."

That startled her. She started to say something sharp, then thought the better of it.

"I don't think he thinks in those terms. He—he—" She shut her eyes against the sudden, embarrassing pain that she'd never expected to show to a total stranger. "He's never had anyone to lo—"

The word *love* wouldn't come out, she found, agonized. Besides, this was not the way to go at it—the problem was somewhat simpler.

"He's never even had any homemade soup," she blurted, "and Martha White baking powder biscuits. Until I fixed them for him."

Augustus Prine considered this.

"Ah," he said, nodding.

She felt like an idiot. "You mean you *understand*?"

"That he hasn't had much fun in life? That's pretty easy to read. I suppose he also not only backs away from commitment, he doesn't even know what commitment *is*." He nodded again, wisely. "Virgin territory, if you don't mind my saying so. But at least it's viable. Young Lancelot just needs to be told."

"Told?"

Augustus Prine clasped both her hands between his.

"That he's in love with you," he said simply. "What else?"

Felicity jerked her hands away and jumped up from the couch.

"You're way off the mark! Oh, why am I telling you this?" She paced back and forth. For some reason, this rather mysterious book salesman seemed to draw things out of her. "We're worlds apart. It's hopeless. Look," she cried, "he's gone back to his former fiancée, the one he was dancing with tonight."

At that moment she saw the white flash of automobile headlights as someone turned into her driveway. She stopped, hesitated, and looked at the man on the couch.

Augustus Prine consulted his wristwatch

"It's after midnight," he said in answer to her unspoken question. "You're not expecting anyone?"

At that hour? Felicity's life was too boringly predictable for that.

She shrugged. "They're probably just turning around."

But she was wrong. The car stopped, the engine was cut and the headlights turned off. They heard footsteps approaching the house, coming around the back to the kitchen door.

That broke the spell.

"I'll get it." She had a feeling something terrible was about to happen.

Felicity raced across the living room, through the door to the breakfast area and half closed it behind her. Someone was already impatiently pounding on the back door.

When she threw the back door open Felicity gasped.

"Oh no," she whispered.

Michael Hanks, his handsome face rosy with November cold, stepped into her kitchen. Felicity had an odd thought as she looked at him. She wondered why she'd ever thought men with fleshy faces and deep dimples in their chins were devastatingly handsome. But she couldn't open her mouth.

"Good. You're home," Michael said, irritably. "I figured if I came late enough I'd get you after your date or whatever it is." He craned to see through the half-opened door to the living room. "Look—I've got to talk to you. When did you begin to date somebody? Who is he? Do I know him?"

"Uhh—" Felicity's mind was still registering that Michael Hanks had driven sixty miles to Griffin from Atlanta to see her at this hour of the night. Michael was married. With a new baby. He had no business there.

"Y-you can't talk to me now," she managed.

"Felicity, don't you know what all this means to me?"

He gazed down at her with somber brown eyes, making an appeal that had always been effective as long as she'd known him. *Michael with a problem*, she labeled his look. You were supposed to be flattered, Felicity remembered, that big, educated, good-looking Michael Hanks, high-school principal and counselor to literally hundreds of young people, would seek you out for *your* advice. Plus your time and attention.

Now he looked impatient. "Don't you see how important this is, that we talk about—*us*? Is that your date? How quick can you get rid of him?"

Felicity blocked his way to the living room.

"Actually, Michael, I don't want to get rid of him." She knew she wasn't being forceful enough; she never was around Michael. She also knew Augustus Prine could hear every word.

But she did know the last thing she wanted was Michael Hanks in the living room together with the all-too-clever, ultraperceptive book salesman.

"Can you—can you—just stay in the kitchen a minute?" Felicity waved him toward a kitchen counter stool. "Actually I think he said he's just going— Oh *no!*"

Another car had pulled up in the darkness outside, its headlights raking the side of the house before it came to a stop behind Michael's Dodge Regal and Augustus Prine's Lincoln town car.

"Wait," she cried.

Her brain was spinning; a strange intuitive sense told her she was entering yet another twilight zone of mayhem. It was after midnight. Three cars in her driveway at this hour? Nothing like this had ever happened in all the years she'd lived in her staid neighborhood in the suburbs of Griffin.

Maybe it was the police, she thought, irrationally. Her house *was* filling up rather nightmarishly with people at this odd hour of the morning.

Her house, she corrected herself, was filling up with *men*.

She was actually too tired to figure it out.

"Stay here." She pushed Michael Hanks out of her way as she started for the living room. "I'll get rid of everyone."

And you, too, after that, she added silently.

In the other room Augustus Prine rose from the couch, tall and darkly sophisticated in his black tuxedo.

"Would you mind stepping into the bedroom?" Felicity waved one arm to show him the way as she hurried to the front door. "First door on your right. Just until I see who this is."

She was suddenly filled with a strange foreboding. Hadn't she told herself many times in the past few weeks that she felt something—she didn't know what—might happen? And she wouldn't know how to handle it if it did?

She threw open the front door. The light from the cozy firelit living room fell on another figure in a tuxedo—tall, leanly muscular, with a square-jawed face, brilliant azure eyes and a shock of disorderly gold hair.

Steven Cambridge was standing on her porch. He'd had to come through the untrimmed althea bushes because the front entrance was hardly ever used, and he looked a little out of sorts. There were a few fragments of green leaves on his shoulders. But those blue eyes were brooding, intense, uncertain.

"You think I'm a fool for doing this," he said, abruptly. "Coming here like this."

He's left his date at the club, was all Felicity could think. *Or he took her home early. To come here....*

Dazed, Felicity nearly staggered backward.

Steven Cambridge had come to her. He really had! But she had men hiding in the bedroom, she remembered frantically, in the kitchen. And they were listening.

"Lyla and I," Steven Cambridge was saying, "know it won't work now, after tonight. It just isn't there, in fact, it never was. You know who Lyla is, don't you?" he said, frowning.

Felicity could only nod, numbly.

He's here, she repeated to herself in a state of shock. *I don't really want him. I ought to send him away. He doesn't love me. He just wants sex and a fancy home-cooked breakfast.*

But if her brain wasn't working, her treacherous heart was. And it was melting.

Steven Cambridge ran his hand through his gilded hair in a gesture that was, for him, surprisingly awkward.

"I don't know what it is," he muttered. "I'm rotten with interpersonal relations, women always tell me that. It was the way I was raised, the way I live. I suppose it's hell on other people." He looked around almost furtively. "It's cold out here on the porch. May I come in?"

No! Felicity's mind cried.

But she stepped aside.

He moved into the living room uncertainly. "You and I—" His eyes caught a movement through the half-open kitchen door, but he went on, distracted, "Ever since that night—those nights—at my cabin—I never thought I would be...."

He stopped.

A cold prickling on the back of her neck told Felicity almost without turning that Augustus Prine, curious to see what was going on, had come out of his hiding place in her bedroom and was standing now in the living room behind her.

She also saw the lightning-quick shift of Steve Cambridge's eyes that told her Michael Hanks, too, had emerged from the kitchen.

Too late, the meaning of the hour, where she was— who *they* were—struck her all at once. Along with how Steve Cambridge would see it.

"They just dropped in," Felicity croaked. "I know it's late but . . . They just dropped in," she repeated helplessly.

Even as she spoke, she knew nothing was going to help.

Steve Cambridge's sculpted features froze. The blue eyes iced over with distant shock.

"I see you have company." His lips hardly moved.

As Felicity watched he seemed to retreat from the harried, confused human of a few seconds ago into the stiffly formal, rigid man she knew had been severely wounded, but would choose to die before he would let others see it.

"Quite a lot of company, in fact," he murmured. "Please forgive me." He turned away. "I'm sorry to have bothered you."

"Wait," Felicity told him.

It was hardly a whisper. She was beginning to realize what he'd been trying to say to her.

Ever since those nights in his cabin? That he and one of his former fiancées had finally called it quits? That he was rotten at interpersonal relations, but. . . .

Her heart was tearing apart. In all her life she'd never imagined a moment when she'd be so helpless!

The man she loved opened the door to the front porch.

In a moment he had disappeared into the darkness.

13

AUGUSTUS PRINE came to the Gingerbread House a little before 7:00 a.m., Monday morning, parking his spectacular Lincoln town car in the middle of the circular driveway. Fortunately there wasn't too much traffic at that hour. Felicity was in the big assembly room, sitting on the floor tying Fred Alan Harper's shoelaces, when she looked up and saw him standing there, watching her.

"You make a pretty picture with a child in your lap, Ms Boardman," the book salesman observed, looking down at her from his six feet, four inches. He was wearing an expensive-looking black-worsted business suit, an impeccable white shirt and silk tie and was as perfectly attired as he had been on Saturday night. "And I must say," he added, "it becomes you."

"Shoelaces are my life," Felicity said. The steady regard of those enigmatic black eyes vaguely annoyed her. Especially after what had happened at her house. "Did someone let you in? We're not supposed to have unannounced visitors wandering around a child-care center, you know."

He nodded, agreeably. "I believe the lady said she was the cook."

Augustus Prine had charmed Cloris Jackson into letting him in? Felicity shot him a disbelieving look before she set Fred Alan on his feet.

"Come back to me after lunch nap," she whispered to the child, "and we'll do it again. Shoelaces aren't so hard to learn if you practice a lot."

Fred Alan went off to join his group in the larger playroom. Augustus Prine waited until the child was out of earshot.

"I'm leaving for Savannah." He gave Felicity a helping hand up from the thick-carpeted playroom floor. "But I thought I'd stop by to say I have a little time this morning to, ah, set things straight, if you want me to."

When she turned away from him without replying, the book salesman grinned.

"Hey, consider that it might be worth it, beautiful Ms Boardman. I know you were upset by what happened Saturday night, but from a more objective point of view—mine—I thought that scene in your living room with three of your, ah, gentlemen callers popping in by three separate doors had its genuinely humorous moments. Especially with your friend from Atlanta, Whats-his-name, finally blowing his stack. Isn't he your former fiancé?"

Felicity didn't want to think about the temper tantrum Michael Hanks had thrown when she'd insisted he leave the house with Augustus Prine—and without the cozy problem-solving session he had so obviously wanted to have with her about his marriage. With perhaps an overnight stay in her bed an added option.

When Felicity remained silent Augustus Prine shrugged.

"Anyway, it occurred to me that I could call on young Dr. Lancelot before I leave town and explain that it really was as you said. That we *did* more or less drop in on you the other night. Although I gather I was the only one who really had an excuse, as I brought you home from the party."

Felicity kept her back to him.

"That's not necessary. Look, I appreciate your offer to talk to Dr. Cambridge, that's really very nice of you. But I don't need anybody to testify to my innocence. I'm certainly not interested in anyone who would really believe I was entertaining *two* men in my home late Saturday night for—for . . ." Her anger overwhelmed her.

"Immoral purposes?" Augustus Prine's mouth quirked irresistibly. "That sort of thing might be a little speedy for Griffin, Georgia, Ms Boardman. Actually, my impression was that the good doctor was pretty racked up, like any man who finds two other dudes hanging around his woman. He'd showed up on your doorstep to tell you something pretty important. What was it?"

Felicity picked up a stack of nap blankets from the top of the built-in cubbyholes that contained the children's belongings during the day, and carried them over to the work table to count and smooth them out. She'd forgotten Augustus Prine had been standing in her living room listening all that time.

She lifted a nap blanket, shook it out and folded it again, unnecessarily. "Nothing important," she muttered. "Actually Steve Cambridge didn't really have anything to say. He never does."

"The hell he didn't," the big man rumbled. "I heard him say something about ever since that night at the cabin he hasn't been able to get you out of his mind."

The wobbly pile of blankets slipped off the surface of the table and fell to the floor. Felicity stared at them. This man knew more than was good for her nerves. Why didn't he just go away?

"Just what is your interest in all this, Mr. Prine?" she said, facing him squarely. "Look, I don't know you, I never met you before the night before last! Why are you so concerned with what goes on between Steve Cambridge and me?"

The book salesman stood looking at her quizzically. It was a long moment before he answered.

"Let's just say, Ms Boardman," he said quietly, "that if you ever decide Dr. Lancelot isn't the man, you'll let me know."

She looked up and met those coal-black eyes.

Augustus Prine meant what he said, Felicity thought, and it was more than she was prepared to deal with at that moment. Somewhat dazedly she was aware for the first time that she, Felicity Boardman, who had barely survived Michael Hanks's jilting her days before their intended wedding two years ago, now had three men she was more or less involved with. Augustus Prine had just made his stand pretty clear. Good heavens, she wondered, how had this happened?

He was watching her closely. Then his expression changed, became resigned.

"But I expect," he drawled, "that your mind is already made up on that subject. Isn't it?"

Was it? Felicity could hardly think. But deep down in her heart of hearts she knew Augustus Prine was right. She wouldn't change her mind. Not about Steve Cambridge—and no matter what crazy things kept happening to them.

Augustus Prine reached into his inner suit pocket and drew out a business card, holding it out to her between two fingers. "You sure you don't want me to stop by the doctor's office and do a little explaining about night before last, and all the company you had at your house?"

Felicity took the business card from him. She stared down at the printing that gave his name, the name of his publisher and his Macon address. Augustus Prine, she decided was a very nice person.

Felicity took a deep breath. She suddenly felt better because she knew what she was going to do. Somehow she had to go to Steve Cambridge and talk to him. *Really* talk to him.

"I'll take care of it," she told him decisively, "myself."

"'Atta girl." He was solemn for a moment, then he grinned his big, piratical grin. "See me to the door?"

Felicity picked up the blankets from the floor and stacked them with a firm hand. She grinned back at him. "It's the least I can do."

IN THE NEXT HOUR Felicity kept herself busy, along with Iris and Cloris Jackson, taking the children as they arrived and getting them out of bulky cold-weather clothes, checking out any important details from rushed mothers trying not to be late for work and, cautiously, looking for more signs of blossoming mumps.

"I can't believe we're in the clear," Felicity muttered as almost the last child went off to the dining room to get a glass of milk and a bowl of hot cereal. "Unless we strike out with the latecomers, we haven't got one fresh case."

She was interrupted by the squeal of tires in the driveway as Carl Calhoun drove his pickup truck in at breakneck speed, then jammed on the brakes. *Late, as usual,* Felicity thought as she held the door open.

Dennis, holding his father's hand, seemed strangely subdued. His blue eyes were heavy-lidded, sleepy. His everyday bruises, though, seemed to be fading except for a fresh purple one exposed by his rolled-up sleeves that covered most of his arm from wrist to elbow.

"He don't feel good this morning." Carl, his hard, good-looking face reddened with cold, towered over them looking a little worried. "Dennis didn't eat his breakfast, either."

Felicity and Iris converged on the little boy so suddenly their heads bumped.

"Will you let me do it?" Felicity said irritably.

Iris stepped back as Felicity undid Dennis's coat. She heard Dennis's father say something to her assistant in an undertone, but Felicity couldn't make out all the words. It sounded as though Carl was inviting Iris out to a movie. Iris kept one frightened eye on what Felicity was doing.

Her assistant needn't have been so nervous; Felicity was looking for mumps. She'd also made a note of the bruise that Carl had explained away by saying Dennis fell out of a tree in their backyard.

Carl and Iris had been doing more than just sociable dating, Felicity knew that by now. Too many mornings, lately, Iris had arrived looking dreamy and blissfully tired, her mouth slightly swollen and her hair needing a touch-up with electric curlers. In other words, Iris had that generally muted, blooming air Felicity always connected with a woman who'd spent the night making love.

She hoped Carl and Iris were discreet and went to bed together when Dennis was safely in his. Still, there was a certain danger. If Dennis's mother should ever come back and want to claim him, an unmarried relationship with another woman wouldn't make Carl Calhoun look very good in the eyes of a custody judge.

In addition to all the other things one could suspect him of, Felicity thought rather grimly.

"This feel sore?" She felt under Dennis's ears and in his throat with gentle fingers. Dennis shook his head, no, but in slow motion. "How much sleep did you have last night, Dennis?" Felicity asked rather sharply. She heard Carl occasionally rented videotapes of old movies and let Dennis sit up half the night with him watching terrible things like *Night of the Living Dead*. No wonder Dennis had nightmares.

Dennis looked at Felicity with listless eyes. "Birds," he said with only the ghost of his usual energy. "I got birds."

"Lord, don't start that bird stuff," his father said behind him. "That's all that boy talks about. That and those little blue Smurfs. Come give me a kiss, son, I gotta go to work."

Dennis kissed his father, who passed him over to Iris before Felicity could field him. But she saw the look the black-haired construction worker gave her assistant.

Felicity sighed. She was definitely going to have to talk to Iris, too.

ALL THROUGH the busy morning Felicity kept telling herself she would take time to call Steven's office just any minute.

But she hesitated.

How was she going to make it work, anyway, this resolution of hers to see things through with him? She couldn't call him up on the telephone and simply state that they needed to talk. Especially not after Saturday night. He'd probably refuse to speak to her, Felicity thought wavering again.

She had to have a plan. It had reached a point where action was required; she couldn't just let things slide; she had to explain. After all, she remembered with pleasure that Steve Cambridge had come all the way to her house Saturday night with something so urgent it couldn't wait. And she still couldn't believe it, but he'd actually said he had decided it was all over with the beautiful blonde he'd brought to the country club dance!

And yes, she reminded herself, Augustus Prine was probably right. Steve *had* started to say something important about the wonderful two days they had spent together at his cabin at Lake Jodeco. Then everything had fallen apart.

She'd been foolish. Felicity knew now she hadn't handled it well at all. But in all fairness, she supposed if she'd been in Steve Cambridge's shoes and had found the book salesman and Michael Hanks hanging around, she'd have been monumentally turned off, too.

Just after lunchtime, when the children had been settled down for the early-afternoon nap, Felicity found a free moment and went into her office.

This is it, she told herself, squaring her shoulders. She had to pick up the telephone, dial Steven Cambridge's number and ask to speak to him.

But instead of lifting the receiver, she succumbed to an attack of self-doubt. She stood staring at the phone, rehearsing her possible opening lines.

"Steve? This is Felicity Boardman. How's everything?"

Good heavens, not that, she told herself. *He'll have hung up by that time.*

"Steve—don't hang up—this is Felicity Boardman."

More direct, but not much better.

Perhaps she could just leave a message with his secretary to have him call her!

Bad, bad, Felicity immediately told herself. *You know he's not going to return your call, not the way he*

*looked when he left your house. He was devastated.
He's not feeling very friendly toward you now. Again.*

But she had to do it, she thought, taking a deep
breath. Maybe it would work if she burst into hysterical sobs and just started screaming that she loved him.
That was the way she felt; maybe Steven Cambridge
would respond to *that*.

Felicity gnawed her lip. She doubted it, but if he
could come all the way to her house to say what he'd
said—and she knew that had cost him a lot—then she
ought to be able to put her pride in her pocket and do
this.

"Steve, I love you," she murmured, experimentally.
"Please don't hang up on me."

That was what she should say, she supposed. As if in
a dream, Felicity lifted the receiver. She dialed the
number she had before her.

"Doctor Cambridge's office," a voice answered
crisply.

"I'd, ah..." Felicity felt cold flashes of fear run up and
down her legs and into her spine. "I'd like to speak to
him, please."

"I'm sorry, but the doctor is out," the crisp voice responded. "Will you leave a message?"

The office door had opened, Felicity noticed. Iris
stood there, waiting for Felicity to finish her telephone
conversation.

"No—yes," Felicity said. She wasn't prepared to find
Steven out when she called; after all that build-up she
felt like a balloon with all the air leaking out.

But another part of her brain was wondering what Iris wanted. Her assistant was just standing there, her big eyes fixed on Felicity in what seemed like an urgent, mute cry for her attention.

"When will he be—never mind." It was useless to go any further with Iris standing there looking that way.

Felicity hung up.

As she lifted her head she knew before Iris spoke that something was wrong. Terribly wrong. She could feel it in the icy cold fear that coursed through her veins.

"It's Dennis," Iris said in a dread whisper. "We can't wake him up from his nap."

14

Time was supposed to fly in times of great stress and misfortune, but the hours after little Dennis was carried out of the child-care center were some of the longest Felicity'd ever spent in her life.

It was well after six o'clock when Felicity got away from the Gingerbread House and joined Iris at Griffin Memorial Hospital. She was directed to the third floor, the hospital's X-ray section, where Dennis Calhoun was, hours later, still under observation.

Felicity took the elevator with wobbly legs. It was just unbelievable that anything could happen to their tousle-headed "Dennis the Menace." And yet, she thought with a burst of remorse, hadn't they all accepted that *something* would happen eventually to their rambunctious, accident-prone child? Perhaps they could have done more to prevent it. Had they turned a blind eye to what was really going on? Perhaps whatever had happened could have been avoided, Felicity fretted. Maybe Dennis could have been taken away from his abusive father, if what everybody suspected was true.

If that's what's happened I'll always blame myself, she was thinking as the elevator doors opened onto the glaring white-enameled corridors of the X-ray department.

She almost didn't recognize her assistant, who sat huddled on an oak bench farther down the hall. Iris looked so small and forlorn.

When she saw Felicity she jumped up and started toward her. For a moment Felicity thought Iris was going to throw herself into her arms and burst into tears. Instead, she turned away, her face bleak.

"He's got a concussion," she said dully, "and maybe other head injuries. They've called Dr. Cambridge in because they want a neurosurgeon to look Dennis over. It took a while to get him—he was at his cabin at the lake."

Felicity had to sit down as her legs would no longer hold her upright. She sank onto the hard wooden bench.

"Not mumps, then."

Iris stared at her.

Felicity knew it was crazy, but she'd been clinging to the hope that Dennis had simply succumbed to their mumps epidemic. That this was some virulent strain that would knock even their two-legged bombshell into a prolonged state of unconsciousness. She'd been grasping at straws.

Felicity had closed up the Gingerbread House alone that evening. In the hours since the ambulance had taken Dennis away no one had called the center to tell her anything. The two times she'd managed to get to the telephone to call the hospital, patient information was notably uncommunicative. Dennis was in X-ray, was all the operator would say, and his condition was "guarded."

"Where's Carl?" she wanted to know. They'd called Dennis's father from the Gingerbread House at the same time they'd called the ambulance.

"At the pay phones in the lounge." Iris indicated the direction with her head. "He's been there for almost an hour this time, trying to get ahold of Dennis's mother." Iris did not conceal the bitterness in her voice. "So far we don't think she's in the state of Georgia. The people he's called think her new husband's been transferred to some Navy base in California."

Felicity felt a pang. Poor Dennis. Hadn't she told herself not so long ago that part of his behavior problem was that he missed his mother? It looked as though he wasn't going to have her even now, when he was lying unconscious in the hospital.

"I keep thinking we should have done something," Felicity groaned.

"Like what?" Iris's expression was hostile. "You mean, make Carl take Dennis down to the clinic the way Myra Bates wanted him to do? To be worked up as a possible child-abuse case?"

"Oh, Iris, will you stop being so—"

Felicity didn't finish as the elevator doors opened a few feet away from them and the tall, graceful figure of Dr. Steven Cambridge appeared.

For the first few feet he didn't see Felicity and Iris sitting on the bench in front of the doors to the X-ray complex. He had his head down, his expression closed and abstracted as he strode toward them wearing a black wool turtleneck sweater that emphasized his leanness and his broad shoulders, tight-fitting worn blue jeans, and boots. He looked as though he had just come straight from a relaxing day off, at his lakeside cabin. And now he was in a tearing hurry.

When he saw Felicity he slowed his pace just a fraction, his eyes darkening with some unfathomable expression. But he passed them at a fast lope and slammed through the swinging doors.

"He was almost running," Iris said, coming to her feet. "Oh, my Lord, do you think Dennis is worse? There must be some sort of emergency—"

"He always runs." Felicity took Iris's arm and drew her back down on the bench. "I mean it, he's the most restless, high-energy man I've ever known. He never does anything at normal speed."

Felicity was remembering the cold, crisp days at Lake Jodeco and Steven Cambridge running around the lake with his hands held out in front, elbows clasped to his sides to minimize the pain. She pulled herself back to the present with an effort.

"If someone would just tell us something," Iris moaned. She nodded at the nurse's station at the far end of the hall. "They won't tell me anything because I'm not a member of the family. It's just terrible to sit here and think of that poor baby lying unconscious—"

"Stop it, Iris."

Felicity spoke it more severely than she'd intended. But if she kept it up Iris would have her in tears. And this was no time for both of them to go to pieces.

"Did he say anything. . . ." Felicity desperately tried to make conversation. Ask about facts. "Did Dennis say anything this morning that might indicate what was wrong? Did he say he fell?" *Or that his father struck him*, she couldn't help adding mentally.

"Only about the birds." Iris was distracted; she kept watching the X-ray department's swinging doors. "Dennis always talks about the birds. And the tree."

"What tree?"

"I don't know," the other woman murmured. "The tree the birds live in, I guess. I can't follow what Dennis says, he doesn't talk all that well most of the time."

They saw Carl Calhoun approaching from the other end of the hall and the visitor's lounge. He walked slowly, dragging his big, booted feet, the picture of discouragement.

He nodded to Felicity. "No luck," he said. "Nobody knows where she's gone." His lips tightened. "When my kid wakes up and cries for his mother, I guess he'll know this time she's long gone. And won't come back."

"Don't say that," Iris cried.

He glowered down at her. "We're better off without her. She doesn't give a hoot about Dennis, I don't care if she never comes back, and that's the truth. A dozen of her's not worth one of you, Iris," he said somberly. "You've cared more for my boy than she ever did."

Tenderly Iris put her arms around Carl Calhoun's body and held him, her head resting against his chest. Carl rested his chin in Iris's blond hair, looking tired and sad. They were so absorbed in each other they seemed to forget Felicity sitting right before them.

"I'll talk to him when he wakes up," Iris promised. "He's used to having me around, maybe that will be just as good as having his mother."

"*If* he wakes up," his father said, still grim. "The doctors still don't know why he's unconscious, that's why they called the neurosurgeon."

Felicity was so involved in this totally new, tender play of emotion between her child-care assistant and Carl's father that she jumped violently when the swinging doors to the X-ray rooms flew open again.

It was Steven Cambridge. She'd never seen him in hospital clothes, and he was transformed. He wore a green jacket and green wrinkled operating room trousers and faded green canvas shoes. A stethoscope flapped around his neck. He looked impatient. That was familiar. The furious scowl was familiar, too. The moment he saw Carl Calhoun he started for him.

Horrors—*that* was familiar, too!

The last time Felicity had seen Steve Cambridge going for someone that way was in her driveway the chaotic night of their date.

"Steve—wait!" she cried, jumping to her feet. Carl was a brawler; he'd chew him up and swallow the pieces!

But the tall construction worker was completely taken by surprise. He actually held out his hand as Steven Cambridge rushed toward him.

"Doctor Cambridge?" was all he got to say.

The next moment Doctor Cambridge had slammed him against the corridor wall in a furious body tackle. Then he had him around the throat.

"You murdering slime," Steve was shouting. "He's only a damned baby! How about picking on somebody your size!"

Iris screamed. Felicity stood frozen. For a lightning second she remembered being on the telephone with Iris in his cabin, and Steve overhearing some of her conversation about Carl's supposed drinking.

"Hey!" a startled Carl yelled as the neurosurgeon grabbed his hair with both hands and slammed his head against the wall. "Hey, Doc, what the hell's the matter with you?"

Felicity could hardly hear Steven Cambridge's growled answer.

Iris was running in circles around the two struggling men, screaming at the top of her lungs. Iris looked as though she was looking for a place to hit Steven Cambridge that would make him loosen his hold on Carl Calhoun's throat.

Felicity started for Iris, aware that two white-clad figures were running down the hall toward them from the nurse's station. Dimly she heard hospital alarm bells ringing.

"Iris, don't hit him," Felicity cried as Iris brought her fist down in the middle of Steven Cambridge's back.

He hardly noticed. At the moment he was recklessly pummeling Carl Calhoun's face and head, shouting, "I'm writing you up for child assault, goon! You know what they do to child abusers in jail? You know what other felons do to them?"

"Hey man." Carl tried to back away. His lip was bleeding. "You nuts or something?"

"Steve!" Felicity pushed Iris away with both hands. "Will you stop hitting him?" she screamed.

But in some quieter part of her mind Felicity knew what was happening. The demons were back. Nothing was quite as raucously insane as the things that happened when she and Steven Cambridge were together. If only she could keep him from beating Carl into insensibility. Or Carl got over his surprise and decided to cream Griffin's star brain surgeon!

Fortunately at that moment the elevator doors opened on the X-ray floor again to the clanging of alarm bells. Two uniformed City of Griffin policemen came running out.

"Watch it, Steve!" Felicity shouted.

It was too late. Carl Calhoun had seen the cops, too. He swung widely, desperately, and caught Dr. Steven Cambridge squarely on the chin.

Felicity was horrified as the figure in hospital greens caromed off the wall and then slid to the floor.

"You—you—" she spluttered at Carl Calhoun.

She angrily charged and swung her pocketbook. It hit him a resounding whack on the side of the head.

Dazed, Dennis's father stumbled into the arms of a policeman. "What have I done?" he cried. "Whatcha all beating on me for?"

One uniformed policeman tenuously held a struggling, screaming Iris by the arm, keeping her from coming to Carl's aid. Felicity picked up her pocketbook. The floor where Steven Cambridge was seated, gingerly rubbing his chin, was littered with her spilled pens, notebook, lipstick, keys and the rest of the contents of her bag.

"Are you all right Dr. Cambridge?" one of the RNs called.

Felicity turned and glared at her. From his seat on the floor Steven Cambridge looked up at the two policemen and a baffled Carl Calhoun they held between them.

"I'll tell you what you've done," Dr. Cambridge snarled. "I'm reporting you for child abuse. One look at that kid in there and there's no other conclusion. He's been beaten."

15

IT SEEMED LIKE only a few minutes later that Felicity got to her knees and searched under the X-ray department's wooden bench for the last of her scattered things that had spilled when she swung at Carl Calhoun with her pocketbook. In actuality it was more like half an hour.

And what a half hour, she thought wearily.

The two policemen who had answered the X-ray department's call for help had taken Carl Calhoun down to Griffin's central police station to be booked not on child-abuse charges—an angry Dr. Steven Cambridge hadn't done the paperwork on that, yet—but on charges of attempted assault and disorderly conduct. Iris had followed the police car, determined to get the always-strapped-for-cash Carl a lawyer and post bail for him if necessary.

The trouble was, Iris had about as little money as Dennis's father, so Felicity had given Iris a check on her own bank account for fifty dollars. Which left all of them, she thought ruefully, pretty broke.

On her hands and knees, Felicity peered under the bench. She was looking for her pocket comb and second-best lipstick that were still missing.

Now that things had quieted down, she knew that all the trouble probably wouldn't have erupted if Steve Cambridge had given Carl half a chance to find out what was going on. Carl's punch that floored the doctor—witnessed by the police—seemed to be due more to confusion and a need to protect himself than anything else. Now Carl was under arrest.

Felicity was learning that nothing was going to stop Steven Cambridge once he got into his "tiger" mode. Good heavens, the man was not only high-strung and restless, he had a trigger temper, too! She should have learned *that* when he'd demolished Walter Kendrick with judo chops and karate.

More and more she was beginning to understand why Steven Cambridge had been engaged several times but had never gotten married. Felicity had always supposed that something was lacking in the women he'd become involved with. It had never occurred to her that not only did Steve have a strangely distant and uncommunicative personality, he kept getting into fights, too! It was a strange combination.

Felicity found her comb and lipstick against the back wall, fished them out from under the bench and got to her feet.

Violence had erupted when Steve Cambridge had come charging out of X-ray, assuming that Carl Calhoun was guilty of child abuse. But the two policemen had pointed out that no one knew this to be true because there hadn't been an investigation. And there was, so far, no proof of anything.

True, Dennis was in the hospital with suspected head injuries, but an angry Carl Calhoun maintained his son had fallen out of a tree in their backyard. Dennis, he'd told them, was crazy about birds and was always climbing the tree no matter how many times Carl warned him not to.

Steve Cambridge still didn't believe him. But Iris did, and she was going to defend Carl to her last ounce of strength. She had gone down to the police station to wait while Carl was being booked on assault charges and then she was going to try to bail him out.

"Did you get everything?" a voice said behind her.

Felicity turned. It was Bonnie Dixon, head nurse in X-ray and also mother of Tiegan Dixon, one of the Gingerbread House's four-year-olds.

"I think so." Felicity brushed off her knees with one hand. "But I feel like I just got caught in between Mike Tyson and his sparring partner. Were you here when all that was going on?"

"Who wasn't?" the head nurse said. "Word got out that our wonder-man Steve Cambridge was beating up on some suspicious character in X-ray, and I think the whole hospital turned out. We didn't hear that it was the kid's father he was tearing into. Steve's got quite a reputation," she added, looking at Felicity thoughtfully, "for being hotheaded. You wouldn't think it to look at him, he's such a gorgeous hunk, but you should see him operating. He terrorizes the OR nurses. You'd think they'd want to kill him, but they don't. They actually idolize him. They see the things he does in brain surgery, the impossible stuff, and they all think he's a god."

Felicity stared. That was quite a testimonial. "He *has* got a trigger temper," she murmured.

Bonnie Dixon snorted.

"That's putting it mildly. They had to pry him off Buck Whitehead, the anaesthesiologist, one morning because Steve thought Buck had screwed up during a cranial exploratory, and he wasn't going to give him the benefit of the doubt. With Stevie-boy, everything's black and white. And you'd better do an award-winning performance or you're going to regret it. It's hell on OR teams, but it gets results." She looked at Felicity out of the corner of her eye. "You've dated him, haven't you? I've always thought Steve Cambridge ought to get committed, have a really energetic sex life, lots of TLC—that should take some of the heat off the people he works with."

Felicity turned bright red.

Great, she told herself, gritting her teeth. So the hospital staff wanted Steve Cambridge to have a sexy affair so they could get their temperamental genius off their backs! And the great doctor himself was apparently looking for an arrangement that provided an above-average romp in bed and good food! Was there anything about being in love with Steven Cambridge, she wondered, that didn't sound like a doctor's prescription?

Take as indicated: one sturdy, sexy woman companion with great staying power and superior culinary skills for affair with difficult but brilliant brain sur-

*geon. Administer expert ballroom dancing, home-
made soup, inspired lovemaking, some jogging,
occasional wood chopping. Repeat until he comes to
your house saying something incoherent about those
two nights you spent at his cabin.*

Felicity suddenly felt exhausted.

"The one thing I'd really like to do before I leave," she
said, thinking longingly now of a quiet evening at home
in front of the television with a good microwaved TV
dinner, "is take a peek at little Dennis Calhoun. But I
don't suppose that would be possible."

"I don't see why not," the nurse said. "The kid with
suspected head injuries? They did a spinal tap and he's
been moved to intensive care."

"But they won't let me in intensive care," Felicity told
her.

Bonnie Dixon smiled.

"Yes they will. They've even got pediatric beds in ICU
with windows so the parents can see without getting in
the way of treatments. Nobody will bother you if I call
down and tell them to let you in."

IT WAS SHORTLY after the hospital dinner hour by the
time Felicity got to the intensive care unit. The hall-
ways were filled with food carts, and she had to squeeze
between them looking for the bank of windows at the
children's rooms.

She went from one glass panel to another. Most of
the rooms were empty, except for one dimly lighted
room where Dennis Calhoun lay in a big standard-size
hospital bed that overwhelmed his small wiry body.

Felicity leaned up against the soundproof window and rested her forehead on the glass. It all looked so still, so ominously calm. The very small boy in the big white bed didn't move; she could hardly believe it was their perpetual-motion "Dennis the Menace" in there. There were tubes in his arms and nose, and his eyelids were closed and blue-veined. Someone sat with him, just outside of the pool of light of the bedside lamp, in partial shadow.

Steven Cambridge, she realized, with a start of surprise. His elbow was propped on the bed beside the child, and his chin rested in his open hand. The light gilded his fair hair and his carved features. His eyes were closed. One long-fingered hand held Dennis's wrist, monitoring his pulse.

Neither one of them moved, not the small, still child nor the man sitting by the bed. They'd been like this for some time, Felicity knew.

A sudden, painful lump rose in her throat.

A hospital attendant pushed a food cart full of rattling metal trays up behind her and stopped, watching the quiet tableau on the other side of the window.

"He does that," the woman offered, "that Doctor Cambridge. If it's some kid he's operated on, he comes into ICU and sits with them. He won't let nobody else do it. You come here any hour of the day or night and he's sittin' there dozing, it looks like. But the nurses say he knows what's going on even if it doesn't look like it."

Felicity's eyes suddenly filled with tears. She kept her face turned away.

Steven Cambridge was a difficult, temperamental tiger. And when he wasn't distant and turned off, she gathered he was a hothead and a hell-raising perfectionist at work. He also knew he didn't do well in close personal relationships—wasn't that what he'd mumbled on her doorstep?

But he was also an angel, she told herself wistfully, who sat by sick kids' beds at all hours, night and day, in ICU when the nursing staff could have been doing it. And when he looked so tired he could fall off the chair.

And she loved him.

Tears spilling unashamedly down her cheeks, Felicity reached into her purse for a handkerchief. The hospital attendant patted her comfortingly on the shoulder.

"Don't you worry, lady," she said. "If Dr. Cambridge is looking after your little boy, he's going to be all right."

Felicity didn't bother to correct her.

Beyond the glass they saw Steven Cambridge stir and open his eyes. That bright blue gaze was tired, unfocused for a moment in the dim light of the intensive care room. Then he looked up at the window, as though he expected to find someone watching him. His eyes settled on Felicity.

If he was surprised to find her standing there at the window he didn't show it. As for Felicity, the impact of those eyes was always like being plugged into a bolt of storm electricity. She was glad that he saw her, although his expression said nothing.

With a sigh, she turned away.

16

IT WAS RAINING AGAIN—hopefully the last of the November downpours—as Felicity drove home. December was usually better, she reminded herself, crisp, cold and windy, bright cheerful weather in time for Christmas.

The telephone was ringing as she let herself in.

"Where have you been?" Iris demanded. She sounded exhausted and stressed out, not her usual sunny self. But then it had been a high-stress day for all of them. "I've been trying to get in touch with you since I brought Carl home from the police station. I—we—had to use your money," she said all in a rush. "I'm sorry, Felicity, Carl and I just didn't have enough between us to make his bond."

"That's all right, Iris, that's what I gave it to you for. I'm just glad Carl didn't have to spend the night in jail."

Or I guess I am, Felicity added silently, trying to give him the benefit of the doubt as to what started this whole thing.

With one hand she slipped off her high heels, unable to keep back a little groan of relief. She padded to the refrigerator, taking the telephone with her.

"*You* get some rest, Iris," she said pointedly. She'd bet anything, Iris was already planning to have Carl spend the night with her. "We have a workday tomorrow, regardless, and a whole bunch of kids coming back who've had the mumps. It's going to be Crankyville time at the Gingerbread House, you know that. Where's Carl now?"

"He's gone home to change his clothes and get something to eat," Iris said guardedly, "and then he's going back to the hospital. He has to, at least until there's some change in Dennis's condition. He's so upset! I know you don't think he's upset, Lissy, you and that doctor think Carl did something terrible to Dennis, but it's not true!" Her voice rose. "Dennis fell out of that oak tree he's always climbing at home. He's told me about it at the Gingerbread House. Carl has told him to stay out of the tree and away from those damned birds he thinks he sees, but you can't explain that to anybody. Carl tried down at the police station, but I saw their faces—they didn't believe him, either, their minds were already made up. They looked like they wanted to kill him right there!"

Abruptly Iris burst into sobs.

Felicity got a fried chicken dinner out of the freezer and leaned up against the refrigerator, listening to her assistant crying her heart out. Poor Iris, she thought. We're both in love, and it certainly isn't making either of us ecstatically happy.

"Get some rest, Iris," she told her. "And don't go back down to the hospital tonight." She had a sudden thought. "Good heavens, Carl hasn't gone up to the intensive care unit, has he?"

If Carl and Steve Cambridge tangled again at the hospital they'd *both* land in jail!

"He's not going to bother your Dr. Cambridge, Lissy." Iris's tone was sullen. "Believe me, Carl's got too much to worry about, he doesn't need some crazy at the hospital who wants to beat up on him before he even knows the facts. Poor Carl, he can't even find Dennis's mother to come and be with her own child."

"From what I see," Felicity murmured, "Dennis doesn't miss his mother all that much. He'd rather have you."

There was a silence on the other end.

"I hope so," Iris said softly. "I love that little demon. Oh, if I had him, Lissy, I swear, Dennis would calm down. I think he wants a lot of loving from somebody who might be . . . his mother. Somebody her age, you know, who... Oh, never mind," she said quickly. "Carl and I haven't talked about anything, so this is silly. Look, I want to go over to the Gingerbread House tonight. I have my key, I just wanted to let you know I'd be there for a few minutes. I want to look in the cubbies, where the kids keep their things."

Felicity couldn't imagine what Iris would want with the children's cubbyholes at the Gingerbread House at almost eight in the evening.

"Won't it wait?" She pried the microwave door open with her thumb, and with her other hand peeled the cardboard back from her frozen dinner. "What in the world do you want over at the center at this hour?"

"I'm looking for something," Iris said, mysteriously. And hung up.

FELICITY SETTLED on the couch in her living room, barefoot and in the lush green velvet robe her sister had given her as a Christmas present, her fried-chicken dinner in her lap. But she only poked at her food; she was too tired to eat. There was not much on television, either, she found after flipping the channels with the remote control for a few minutes. She'd looked forward so much to getting home and out of the cold endless rain, and being warm and comfortable, but her thoughts kept turning back to Griffin Hospital and the prospects of Carl Calhoun and Dr. Steven Cambridge meeting in ICU. And starting their grudge match all over again.

That is, Steve Cambridge's grudge match, Felicity reminded herself.

Dennis's father hadn't put up much of a fight in X-ray until the end, with that lucky punch. She wondered if that meant he was too guilty to defend himself, or too innocent to want to fight over something he didn't do.

When the front doorbell rang, Felicity put her chicken dinner down resignedly. It was probably Iris to tell her about her mysterious mission and whatever was in the cubbyholes at the Gingerbread House.

She should have remembered only one person used the overgrown path to the front door. When she threw open the door there was Steven Cambridge, soaking wet, in his shirtsleeves and without a raincoat, shoulders covered with bits of rain-wet leaves from the shrubbery. His expression was a curious mixture of fatigue and a tense, electric tightness.

"Dennis?" Felicity's heart was in her mouth.

"Conscious." The terse word exploded from him. "Concussed but no apparent complicating trauma. Woke up, sat up, started yelling for his daddy." He ran his fingers through gilded, rain-wet hair. "These things happen, the younger the kid the more common it is, babies have great resilience. ICU's got the sides up on the bed, now, trying to keep him in. He's got to be watched for a few hours."

Felicity literally staggered back into the living room, her relief was so great. Or was it disbelief? Was everything really all right?

"Carl," she managed. "He's there with Dennis?"

He scowled. "Yeah. I told the ICU the father could stay until midnight as long as they watched him like a hawk every minute he was there."

Things were better, Felicity realized slowly. Dennis was conscious. Awake. Trying to climb out of his bed in the hospital. Somehow she couldn't get the touching picture of Steve Cambridge sitting by his side in the dim hospital room out of her mind.

And she didn't want to.

"Come in," she told him.

He was already standing in the middle of her living room, dripping water on her rug, so the invitation wasn't necessary. He looked, at the moment, thoroughly tired and as though he didn't really remember why he'd ended up at her house telling her all this.

But Felicity knew.

She put her hands lightly on the front of his soaked white shirt and began unbuttoning it.

"You're wet through to the skin," she murmured. "Have you had anything to eat? Are you hungry?"

Steven Cambridge looked as though he considered having a meal for the first time that day as she peeled his wet shirt from his shoulders and pulled it all the way off.

"Not food," he said huskily. He shivered as Felicity's stroking fingers touched his chest, then dropped to the belt buckle below. "That can wait."

His hands covered hers, stopping them. "There's so much I want to say," he began, with his eyes he appealed to her in considerable frustration. "Damn, I'm not very good at this. That night when I came to your house...."

He stopped. Felicity had unbuckled his belt and pulled down the zipper of his fly. Now she eased the wet serge of his trousers down his narrow hips.

"Mmm-hmm?" Felicity murmured, encouragingly.

He hesitated, distracted.

"Ah—um." His face froze as her fingers dropped across the front of his tightly-stretched black nylon briefs. "Ah, this is ... this is ... you know no woman's ever done this," he managed in a suddenly choked voice. "Don't you?"

Felicity smiled softly. "Done what?"

She had his trousers down around his knees. He steadied himself with one hand on her shoulder as he slipped off his shoes and stepped out of the pants.

"Undressed me," he said hoarsely.

She looked up at him, all that she felt for the man she loved shining in her eyes.

"It's a first for me, too," she said simply.

His reaction showed in his face. "I need you, Felicity," he said.

She gave a small shriek as he bent and scooped her up into his arms, her green velvet robe billowing around them. He headed toward the bedroom, carrying her.

"But, Steve." She clung to him as he lowered her to the bedspread, pulling him down with her. He toppled on top of her. "I wanted to show you how much...."

"I know. You're not going to tell me anything I haven't said to myself a hundred times coming over here." His hard, muscular length, bare except for his silky black underwear, pressed her down into the soft bed. He was breathing hard, his bright blue eyes holding hers. "You haven't even asked me why I came here tonight."

"To tell me about Dennis," Felicity whispered.

He had run the velvet housecoat's long zipper down the front, baring her breasts, the smooth expanse of her belly and the reddish curls below; now he raised up on one arm and bent over her to uncover her legs and pull the emerald green folds out of their way.

"Something even more important than that."

Distracted by the sight of her, he didn't finish. Felicity saw that shock of gilded hair drop to her breast. His teeth and lips took the aching pink bud of her nipple so passionately that she cried out.

"Did I hurt you?" he said instantly.

"No—no!"

She'd buried her fingers in his hair and it was hard to let go. She was flushed, her body already writhing demandingly under him, burning with her desire for this wonderful man. How could she tell him that just the sight of him caressing her breasts made her so lustful she could hardly bear it? It was embarrassing!

He rolled his lean, golden body to one side quickly.

"I want you to make love to me, I didn't mean to stop you. It's just hard for me to leave you alone."

"It *is*?" Felicity already knew, but she was overjoyed to hear him say it. "Oh, Steve, darling, if you wanted me half as much as I want you. . . ."

She raised herself on one elbow to look down into that incredibly handsome face. Maybe it was the different perspective—being so close and leaning over him for a change—but Felicity didn't understand how she could have ever thought Steven Cambridge distant and unfeeling. In fact, she marveled, those handsome features were very vulnerable in their masculine beauty, especially the long tangled black eyelashes over startlingly blue eyes that now looked at her a little confusedly.

"You see, I only wanted to make love to you, this way," she murmured, "because I wanted to show you how I feel."

His face took on a look of sheer pleasure.

"Show me, love," he whispered.

But his features contracted with something like pain as her hand found his hard, silky-soft flesh. She wrapped her fingers around him. When she stroked him, softly, he groaned with what she was doing to him.

Felicity's eyes widened with alarm at the sound, but he grabbed her hand and put it back against him.

"Darling, you've got absolute power over me." He managed a shaky laugh. "Show me what you feel."

Felicity couldn't resist murmuring somewhat wickedly, "Don't worry, I'll be gentle."

His mouth took hers, then, a little roughly. He seized the back of her head to hold her to his ardent caress. Felicity felt herself dissolving in liquid fire. His other hand ran up her hip to the small of her back, smoothing her white skin, fingers trembling with desire and impatience.

She stroked him, feeling against her own body the shudders of excitement that ran through him as his eager lips caressed her mouth, her chin, the pulsing warm hollow of her throat. When Felicity hesitated, thinking to let go of him, he murmured urgently against her mouth not to stop, that it was too wonderful.

The golden man who held her spoke little phrases, disjointed, against her damp shoulder, arms and throat again as he nuzzled them.

"You smell so good, so sweet, so female, I can't get enough of it. After hospitals, operating rooms—" he sighed "—you smell so damned *good.*"

"Steve . . ." she murmured.

"Let me finish." He buried his head against her warm breast. "I lost a little girl about the Calhoun kid's age last week. On the table, in the middle of the operation. I did a tracheotomy in record time, but it was useless, I couldn't save her. It was hell."

Felicity wrapped her arms around him and held him to her breast. She felt him take a long, shuddering breath.

"When I got home that night all I wanted to do was call you." The words were muffled against her soft flesh. "Or come here, to your house, have you put your arms around me, take me to bed. It was something I'd never felt before. Not with any other woman. Damn, I realized I *needed* you," he said vehemently. "Not just to have sex, I needed you to *hold* me, like this. I needed to talk to you."

Felicity stared up at the ceiling of her bedroom. The man whose warm, hard body was pressed so heavily against hers was everything she'd ever wanted. It was impossible, she thought, her heart hammering, but Steve Cambridge seemed to be trying to tell her that he felt something of the same thing.

"Take me into you," he said softly. "I want to be inside you, Felicity, where I belong."

She hesitated only a second, then settled on him, feeling him enter her, big and hard. He took possession of her. There were tears in her eyes, she was so full of her love for him. But she wasn't prepared for the explosion of passion which took her unawares. Her whole body reacted with an outpouring of love as she thrust down on him, crying out. As she collapsed, her loosened hair fell over his face in a red sweet-smelling shower.

"Oh— *Oh!*" Felicity cried. The storm swept over her, wild, thrilling, cataclysmic. If she hadn't been so much in love she would have been mortified.

As the tremors subsided, Steve held her, strong arms wrapped around her, holding her safely.

"Drat," Felicity muttered. She expected him to laugh.

She lifted herself up and looked into his face. It held anything but laughter, she saw.

"That was the most beautiful thing you could have given me," he whispered. "But then you always give me everything so freely, so damned generously. That's what I love about you."

"Like chicken soup?" She was more serious than she let on. "Or a big breakfast?"

"Are you kidding? No . . . I—"

The bedside telephone rang and they both jumped. Felicity grabbed up the receiver. "Hello?"

Steve still held her tightly, his arms wrapped around her waist and shoulders, his leg between hers; it was oddly erotic to be talking to someone on the telephone in such a gloriously naked, sensual state. Surprisingly she wasn't at all embarrassed.

"Lissy!" Iris fairly screamed at her. "I've found them—Dennis's birds! It's all right, he really *did* fall out of a tree. He told me so this morning, but I wasn't listening! But I have them! He showed them to me and I didn't remember. Guess what? They were in his cubby!"

"Iris—" Felicity began.

She knew whatever Iris was trying to say was important, but Steve's marvelously skillful hands were stroking her breasts, then dropping to make long, tantalizing swoops against her tummy and thighs. She was still very aware that their lovemaking had been interrupted; she'd reached her crashing, dazzling fulfillment, but he hadn't.

"Don't you *understand*?" Iris was yelling, "they were there all the time, in Dennis's cubby!"

"W-what were?" The marvelous fingers had caressed their way to the damp core of her sensitive flesh; now she was shivering with fiery response. Steve's azure eyes looked up, teasing her. "Iris, please—out with it! What was in Dennis's cubby and why are you calling me at this hour?"

"The nest with the hatched birds' eggs.... Felicity aren't you listening? Dennis really did fall out of a tree," her assistant went on breathlessly. "He'd been watching the birds in their nest for weeks, I guess. He must have gotten the nest just as the birds flew away. Oh Lissy, we should have listened to him. And Carl—I love that man, Felicity, I *know* he wouldn't abuse Dennis! Oh, Carl's a little impatient and he's smacked Dennis once or twice when Dennis has tormented him almost out of his mind, but I've had a long talk with Carl about it...."

Iris stopped.

"Felicity, I—is someone with you?" she said cautiously.

Felicity had Steve's hand by the wrist, but it was too late; her body was in an uproar of desire.

"Iris," she managed, unsteadily, "I'm glad you called."

Felicity held her laughter back as she struggled with Steve's erotically threatening hands. The news about the bird's nest, the proof that Dennis really had been in a tree as he'd said and had fallen out of it, was joyous news for Iris. For Dennis and Carl Calhoun, too. For all of them.

The man in the bed with her broke free of her grip and grabbed the telephone.

"I'm going to make an honest woman of her," Dr. Steven Cambridge growled into the receiver. He didn't know who he was talking to and he obviously didn't care. "We're going to get married."

Felicity grabbed the telephone, hurriedly. "He means engaged."

He snatched it back. "Not engaged—I've had enough of that. I'm going to marry her, make her my wife, buy a house, move in with her, whatever's necessary. Right away! *Tomorrow*."

He slammed up the telephone.

"That was Iris," Felicity rebuked him. She waited a long moment. "Did you say something about marrying me?" Her heart was in her mouth, but she needn't have worried. "Hadn't you better ask me fir—"

"Yes," he said with the determined expression she had seen so often. "Right after I do this."

He moved his body over her, his smooth skin damp with wanting her. "After I kiss you." His mouth opened over hers, his tongue invaded her, possessed her passionately, until she whimpered. "And make love to you," he muttered huskily.

Felicity wrapped her arms around his neck as he gently parted her legs and slowly entered her.

". . . and after," her slightly trembling lover whispered against her lips, "we visit paradise."

17

"OH PLEASE, please," Felicity groaned as she looked out the window, "don't let it rain on my wedding day! Where's all the bright, sunny weather we're supposed to have these last weeks before Christmas?"

The sky was definitely cloudy and looked as much like rain as any sky Felicity had ever seen. The bare, storm-tossed branches of the trees over the driveway bent and lashed in a fierce northeast wind. When it rained this way, as it sometimes did in the winter, middle Georgia's red-clay country turned into a sea of vivid mud: the gullies flooded and the run-off from the non-absorbent clay soil inundated small towns, highways and city streets.

"If we lived up in Yankeeland, we'd be in for a good snowstorm." Martha Calloway bundled Felicity's billowing tulle veil up in her hands to keep it off the kitchen floor while they waited to be taken to the church. "This wouldn't be rain—it would probably be a blizzard."

The banker's wife, as Felicity's matron of honor, wore a magnificent peach *peau de soie* creation trimmed with white fox that was almost as dramatic as Felicity's wedding gown. But nothing could match the dress Felicity's younger sister—who couldn't come to the wedding because she was eight months pregnant—had sent from Chicago this time.

An antique white satin wedding dress in lush 1890s style with leg of mutton sleeves, an incredibly tiny waist and a lavish six-foot train trimmed with Alençon lace, purchased at one of Chicago's trendiest collector's boutiques on the North Shore. The mellowed sheen of the old satin complemented Felicity's creamy white skin and red hair superbly, while the enormous cloud of shimmering tulle veil with its tiny nose veil of matching lace lent an air of otherworldly, angelic mystery. No one could deny that Felicity Boardman was truly beautiful.

"Rain will ruin your shoes," Iris observed.

As Felicity's other bridal attendant, Iris wore a long, romantic bell-skirted dress in blue that matched Martha Calloway's except for the fox fur trim. It was hard to overlook the modest-sized diamond ring on Iris's left hand as she settled a borrowed silk evening cape around Felicity's shoulders.

"Just in case, Felicity," she added, "I think we'd better find you some rain boots or galoshes."

"I haven't got any galoshes." Felicity watched the gigantic chauffeured stretch Rolls-Royce Harry Tate Calloway had rented in Atlanta maneuver into her driveway. "And, Iris, my rain boots are knee-high. They'll feel terrible under all this satin."

"But those beautiful white silk shoes will *melt*, honey," Martha Calloway joined in, "if you get them wet."

In spite of her words the banker's wife beamed happily. Nothing, not even the weather could dim her joy over one of the most successful marriages she'd ever arranged in twenty-four years of matchmaking. The rented Rolls limo and the wedding reception were a wedding present from Harry Tate and herself. Only mildly forced on Steve and Felicity, after some argument.

While Felicity put on her rain boots, Harry Tate Calloway and the chauffeur came to the back door with large black umbrellas. Minutes later, after a quick sprint through the driveway, Felicity and her attendants arrived at the Rolls, only somewhat sprinkled with raindrops. Felicity settled in the back seat in a billow of satin and cloudy white. Harry Tate and Iris rode the jump seats and Martha settled next to Felicity.

Unfortunately just as the uniformed chauffeur closed the door and got into his driver's seat, it began to pour in earnest.

"My goodness, we just missed that one," Martha Calloway exclaimed. "I hope this downpour shuts off before we get to the church!"

The chauffeur turned to look out the back window.

"If you ladies could get the bride's veil down a little," he said almost apologetically, "so I can see out the rear it would help. It's kind of hard to back a big limo out of a driveway in a lot of rain like this."

Martha obligingly reached over to rearrange Felicity's veil and get it out of the way.

But Felicity had already stiffened in her seat. A strange but familiar foreboding had swept over her like an icy shower of rainwater.

"Wait!" she cried. She knew it was crazy, but she'd just had this hideous, intuitive flash. Abruptly she leaned forward to the tap at the chauffeur behind his panel of glass. "Listen, whatever you do, don't cut up over the lawn on the left because—"

It was too late. The driver had already cut the wheels. There was a sickening crunch from somewhere under the Rolls as it mounted a strip of grass that was the edge of Walter Kendrick's lawn. They heard a horrifying squeal of anguished iron against rock hard steel.

Everyone jumped.

"What the hell was that?" Harry Tate Calloway exploded.

With something like an oath the chauffeur got out of the limousine, opened the big black umbrella and held it over him as he squatted down to see under the Rolls-Royce.

Felicity closed her eyes. The terrible foreboding still had a grip on her. She knew the words almost before the chauffeur spoke them.

"Mr. Calloway," the chauffeur said, coming to the door. He stood in the driving rain; under the black umbrella his young good-looking face was drawn and unhappy. "I'm sorry, but we've had an accident. It looks like we just ran over some kid's brand new bicycle and training wheels. It's stuck under the Rolls about where the transmission is."

Harry Tate Calloway, too, got out of the limousine to look. Just as the front door on Walter Kendrick's porch flew open and a burly figure in sweatshirt and jogging pants shot out.

"What the hell do you think you're doing out there?" Walter's voice bellowed at them through the rain. He stomped angrily across the lawn, spraying geysers of water from the grass. "Hey, that's my kid's brand new bicycle you jackasses just ruined!"

Felicity slumped in her seat. *It was happening!* Life with Steven Cambridge was always like this—demon-ridden and ecstatically wonderful. She might have known her wedding day would be no exception.

Walter stormed up to the tall, gray-clad chauffeur holding the umbrella politely over the portly figure of Griffin's multimillionaire banker.

"Who the hell are you, fancy pants?" Walter demanded unpleasantly of the uniformed driver. "Some weirdo we got in the neighborhood now driving a big un-American car?"

Before the young chauffeur could answer Walter whirled on morning-coated Harry Tate Calloway and glared down at him intimidatingly from his beefy six-foot height.

"And you, old fat boy," Walter snarled. "What the hell— Oh, hello Mr. Calloway."

Walter suddenly gulped, a sickly smile replacing his ferocious expression.

"Ah, going somewhere this morning?" he said, casting furtive looks through the limousine's window to

Felicity, Martha and Iris inside. In spite of the rain, he seemed to be suddenly sweating.

"My—my goodness," he rasped, "you all are mighty dressed up. I mean, doesn't everybody look purty. Let me guess." Walter squirmed his big body, ingratiatingly, like an overgrown puppy. "Oh, ah, somebody getting married?"

Under the big black umbrella, Harry Tate Calloway looked displeased.

"Who're you?" the multimillionaire wanted to know. He squinted at Walter through the rain and frowned. "You look familiar. You work for one of my companies? One of the kaolin clay mining outfits here?"

Walter wriggled again like a fawning, wet pit bull, the downpour soaking his cotton jersey outfit to his body and plastering his hair to his skull.

"Yes, sir, but actually, Mr. Calloway, sir," he said eagerly, "I guess you'd remember what I'm most famous for. I played football, all-American linebacker for Georgia Tech in—"

"Don't remember that," Harry Tate snapped. "But if you played football you can make yourself useful. Get under the car and get that mess out from under the axle."

"Sir?" Walter said, looking stunned.

"You heard me." Harry Tate signaled to the chauffeur to cover him with the big black umbrella as he moved toward the limousine. "We'll all just sit inside the Rolls here until you get it done. But don't take too much time, hear? We're already late."

Iris looked at her wristwatch. "Felicity," she whispered, "Harry Tate's right. We're already running a little late. The weather will slow us up more, and we've run over something."

"Yes, I know," Felicity told her.

The familiar refrain, "We're late," was beginning to sound appropriately like the White Rabbit's refrain out of *Alice in Wonderland*. In fact, this chaos was all too familiar. Felicity had already begun gathering up the voluminous folds of satin and tulle in both hands. Her yellow rain boots looked strange peaking out from under her billowing skirt.

"There's nothing we can do," she said, sighing. "We'll never get cabs in this mess." Felicity had a good idea where this scenario was headed. It was weird but true—if she weren't getting married to Steven Cambridge today it would be enough to make her want to tear her hair out. "We'd better transfer over to my station wagon," she told her bridesmaid. "We can't afford to be any later than we already are."

"I can't seem to budge this thing," Walter Kendrick's muffled voice came plaintively out from under the Rolls-Royce. "Believe me, I'm trying, Mr. Calloway, but—"

"Keep at it, boy," the multimillionaire ordered.

In the back seat, Felicity flung the Rolls's door open and motioned to Martha Calloway to get out first.

The banker's wife hesitated for the briefest of seconds. Felicity slid along the seat to follow, Iris helping with her skirt.

"Oh, this is going to make Harry Tate so unhappy," Martha Calloway complained. "My goodness, all the money that went into hiring this limousine, and the chauffeur, too! Harry Tate wanted your wedding to be so elegant."

Felicity stepped out into the rain in her beautiful wedding gown, hardly flinching. But once they were in the driveway the banker's wife gasped as she saw Felicity's old Dodge station wagon.

"My Lord! What *is* that thing looking out the back window of your car?"

"Well," Felicity said resignedly, holding both her hands over the top of her veil to try to keep it dry as the chauffeur was busy holding the umbrella over Harry Calloway. "That was formerly the Cookie Monster for our Thanksgiving play at the Gingerbread House. But now Iris and I are remodeling it for our new play. It's going to be the Christmas Fairy or Scrooge, we haven't decided which. I can't take it out in this weather." She sighed. "The papier-mâché will completely dissolve. But if we sit close together it won't crowd us too much."

"I'm not sure I know how to drive this thing," the chauffeur muttered once they were safely jammed into the old station wagon. "Isn't this an antique or something?"

"Felicity, your veil is caught in my glasses, honey," Martha Calloway warned, grabbing at it to disentangle the cloud of tulle.

"Well, the heel of your shoe, Mrs. Calloway," Iris told her, "is caught in the hem of my dress. Will you be careful when you move your feet, please?"

"Felicity, sweetheart," Harry Tate Calloway said from the front seat, "how do you make the door to the damned glove compartment stay closed? I can't breathe with this thing right in my stomach."

"Good heavens," Felicity cried, managing to turn and look back as the station wagon slowly and protestingly ground out of her driveway. "You forgot to tell Walter he could quit! He's still under the limousine trying to get Bobby's bicycle out!"

"Good. Keep him busy until we get back," Harry Tate said, satisfied.

As THE STATION WAGON with the transitional figure of the Cookie Monster-Scrooge-Christmas Fairy in the back seat rolled up to the doors of Griffin's First Methodist Church, it was plain they were not the only ones late to the wedding.

A jam of cars had piled up in a large puddle of water that looked to be two feet deep or more, right in front of the church. The driveway to the church was flooded, too. Several vestrymen in formal morning coats were carrying big black umbrellas and wading through the water, trying to help. Dr. Emerson Castelberry, the church's eminent preacher, was in his shirtsleeves in the midst of it all, directing traffic. Several City of Griffin police cars, their red lights twirling, sat stranded in the deluge.

"I've never seen it like this," Martha Calloway marveled. "It must be a record breaker. Harry Tate, how are we going to get this crowd into the church?"

"I'm so glad you wore your rain boots," Iris murmured, as she watched a hundred or so wedding guests trying to wade through the water toward the steps of the First Methodist Church.

Suddenly there materialized in the soggy crowd the big, powerful figure of Carl Calhoun, looking rugged and a little unfamiliar in a tuxedo, carrying an umbrella and looking anxious.

"Honey," Carl said through the window as Iris hastily rolled it down, "I'm going to have to pick you up and carry you in. You don't mind, do you? It's the only way we can get you ladies out in time for the ceremony. Say, what the hell is that in the back?" He peered at the papier-mâché figure behind them.

"Good morning," Dr. Castelberry said coming up beside him. The minister looked cheerful in spite of the knee-deep flood water. "They tell me a stopped-up storm sewer is responsible for all this." He held out his arms to the women in the back seat of the wagon. "Mrs. Calloway. May I do the honors?"

"I think Harry Tate is going to get the chauffeur to carry me," Martha Calloway said a little nervously. "But thanks, anyway."

On the other side of the limousine Carl opened the door and reached for Iris. As the tall construction worker lifted his fiancée in his arms Felicity heard a familiar voice.

"Darling," Michael Hanks shouted over the roar of the rain. "It's still not too late. You can change your mind!" He waded up as the minister stepped aside. "We're working on a legal separation."

Felicity cringed.

Her former fiancé was abruptly shouldered aside as the chauffeur stepped in front of him to assist Martha Calloway. But Felicity could still hear him.

"Felicity, darling," he was yelling, "you don't have to marry this guy, whoever he is. Not when you can marry me if you'll just be patient. Did you hear me, Felicity?"

"Go away, Michael," Felicity cried, desperately. "Go back to your wife!"

In front of them, Harry Tate waded in the water, cautioning the young chauffeur not to drop Martha.

Left alone in the back seat of the Dodge, Felicity watched as people milled around in the rain-swollen gutters in front of the First Methodist Church. She was realizing she didn't have to wait for anyone, actually, to carry her; from toe to knee she was encased in yellow rubber rain boots under her wedding gown. If it meant getting away from Michael Hanks she could lift her satin skirts high enough and wade through this mess.

Suddenly Michael Hanks, looking disheveled in a rain-soaked blue business suit, was before her, holding out his arms.

"Come with me, my darling." The dimples in his cheeks flashed as he smiled at her with all his old hypnotic charm. "My car's just down the street for a quick getaway. Didn't you hear what I've been telling you? I'm here to rescue you, love! A divorce is just around the corner after we work out some sort of property arrangement. Just give me a few months."

Felicity shrank back, lifting a yellow-booted foot protectively.

"Drat, Michael," she cried, aiming at his midsection, "didn't you hear me telling you to beat it?"

She could have used a little help at that moment. If Michael made a lunge for her and tried to pick her up she knew they'd both land in the murky waters swirling around them, because she wasn't going to go with him even if it meant a knock-down-drag-out fight and she ruined her beautiful gown. Good grief, he was stupid, she fumed. There was only one man in her life now!

At that moment Felicity was so glad she was going to marry difficult, gorgeous, brilliant, sometimes-obnoxious and always hard-to-handle Dr. Steven Cambridge she didn't know what to do. If she was ever sure of anything in her life, she told herself with a sudden rush of happiness, she was sure of this!

Felicity braced herself to shove Michael back into the crowd, wedding dress hiked up rather inelegantly around her hips, but she needn't have bothered. There *were* onlookers willing to come to her rescue, she saw with a grateful sigh.

Out of the silver-gray deluge a tigerish apparition, rain streaming from his gilded hair, materialized behind Michael Hanks.

It was help, Felicity realized, but definitely with warning signals!

"Steven!" Felicity screamed.

It was too late.

"Get your hands off my wife," the warriorlike figure in a rain-ruined, gray morning coat growled.

"What the hell . . ." Michael Hanks muttered, turning as a skilled hand fell, not too gently, on his shoulder to yank him aside. "Hey, she's not your wife yet, she's still—"

Dr. Steven Cambridge, Griffin Memorial Hospital's foremost neurosurgeon let out a truly Conan-the-Barbarian infuriated roar as he grabbed former high-school principal Michael Hanks and tossed the former principal in a hip throw up on to the lawn of the First Methodist Church.

Dr. Cambridge then unfolded a large black umbrella and handed it to Felicity. He was breathing hard.

"You don't have any more ex-boyfriends around, do you?" he asked grimly. "I find it somewhat difficult disposing of them standing in three feet of water."

Her eyes like stars, Felicity smiled tenderly at him.

Bless his heart, she was thinking, this beautiful hunk, her future husband, apparently thought she was the belle of Griffin, Georgia. With legions of lovers fighting a stand-off operation for her at the very doors of the church! It certainly made up for a lot of things in her past.

But it wouldn't do any harm to let Steve think an army of ex-boyfriends was trying to keep her from getting married, Felicity's wise inner voice advised her, at least for a couple of years or so.

"Steve, calm down," she said, balancing the umbrella over both of them as he picked her up in his arms and navigated the lake in front of the curb. "Michael Hanks means absolutely nothing to me. He's an annoying rat, that's all."

She could see Steve didn't believe her.

His beautiful features were grim. Rain dripped off his long eyelashes. He was magnificent, Felicity mused. She tenderly traced the curve of a wet curl on his neck with her finger as they crossed the squashy lawn and mounted the steps. Carl and Iris were close behind them.

"Steven, put me down," Felicity murmured. "Michael Hanks is married. It's *you* I love. Besides, I can't get married in yellow rain boots."

His iron clutch on her only tightened.

"Hello there," Dr. Castelberry said, beaming at them as they stepped through the door of the First Methodist Church. One of his deacons was helping him on with his surplice. "We have some towels in the vestry, and I've got some volunteers with hot irons in the Sunday school kitchen to help to dry you folks—"

"We're not going to stop," Steven Cambridge said, his jaws clenched. "Not with all these ex-fiancés and boyfriends around trying to interfere. We'll get married wet."

Felicity sighed. When he was in his Viking warrior mode, Dr. Steven Cambridge was virtually unconquerable. But Felicity was getting smarter about these things.

One of the vestrymen stepped in front of them. "You can't carry the bride down the aisle, Doctor," he said.

Unheeding, Steven Cambridge maneuvered Felicity through the opened doors into the sanctuary.

As they stepped into the church the congregation turned to them. *Talk about a variation on the shotgun wedding*, their faces said, *this is a new one!* It was the first time in the history of Griffin, Georgia, that a bridegroom had appeared carrying his bride in his arms, headed for the altar.

"Felicity, honey," Martha Calloway hissed. "As your matron of honor I want to say right now that I can't march along in front of you, and neither can Iris, if Stevie Cambridge is going to act like this and tote you all the way down the aisle of First Methodist Church!"

Felicity nodded.

She was resigned to being married in her yellow rubber rain boots. Steve probably wouldn't give her time to pull them off. But she knew, now, something about how to handle her beloved.

"Darling, put me down," she said as the strains of the organ playing the wedding march from Lohengrin began.

In front of her, her bridesmaid's bouquet clutched tightly, Iris moaned, "Good night, people are staring at us!"

"I know," Felicity acknowledged. "But he's just highstrung. I'll take care of it."

She nuzzled her mouth close to Steven Cambridge's ear where the blond strands of his hair curved wetly but endearingly. She felt him shudder, the muscles in his arms contracting as he held her, but she knew it wasn't from discomfort.

"Darling, I love you," Felicity whispered. "I've already carried the shopping bags up to the cabin. Tonight for our wedding supper it's beef Stroganoff, broccoli souffle and lemon meringue pie."

Dr. Steven Cambridge looked down, distracted, at the vision of loveliness in his arms wrapped in yards of misty tulle veiling. For a long moment he seemed not to have heard. Then he smiled at her, meltingly.

"If I ever see that guy around you again, I'll kill him," he said pleasantly, showing his dazzling white teeth.

But he had definitely thought Felicity's words over.

"You know, come to think of it," he said, all his enduring love in his eyes as he set his bride on her feet, "I'm certain I've never had home-made lemon meringue pie."

COMING IN NOVEMBER FROM

Harlequin Superromance

BOOK THREE OF EVE GLADSTONE'S
Merriman County Trilogy
WOULDN'T IT BE LOVELY
All the sizzle of *One Hot Summer*.
All the intrigue of
After All These Years.

The women of Merriman County have a way of
stumbling over the truth and upsetting the status quo in
the process. Jemma Whiting fought an unfair divorce
settlement in *One Hot Summer*. Sarah Crewes turned
the past topsy-turvy in *After All These Years*.

Now, in *Wouldn't It Be Lovely*, reporter Liz Grady digs
a little too deeply for a newspaper story and discovers
there are two sets of rules operating in the county: one
for the privileged old families of Ramsey Falls—and
another for everyone else. When Liz finds herself
falling for one of the ruling class, lawyer Bradford
Kent, she can only hope that her passion for the truth
and the passion in her heart won't clash....

Watch for *Wouldn't It Be Lovely*.
Coming in November 1989.

SR380-1

Indulge a Little Give a Lot

An irresistible opportunity to pamper yourself with free gifts (plus proofs-of-purchase and postage and handling) and help raise up to $100,000.00 for **Big Brothers/Big Sisters Programs and Services** in Canada and the United States.

Each specially marked "Indulge A Little" Harlequin or Silhouette book purchased during October, November and December contains a proof-of-purchase that will enable you to qualify for luxurious gifts. And, for every specially marked book purchased during this limited time, Harlequin/Silhouette will donate 5¢ toward **Big Brothers/Big Sisters Programs and Services**, for a maximum contribution of $100,000.00.

For details on how you can indulge yourself, look for information at your favorite retail store or send a self-addressed stamped envelope to:

INDULGE A LITTLE
P.O. Box 618
Fort Erie, Ontario
L2A 5I3

ONE PROOF OF PURCHASE

To collect your free gift you must include the necessary number of proofs-of- purchase, plus postage and handling, along with the offer certificate available in retail stores or from the above address.

CHT-1

Harlequin®/Silhouette®